R8000/604

A QUEST SO STRANGE

When Helen Ferguson's father loses his job, the family move from Scotland to Bolton, where Helen gets a job at Langley Mills. There she becomes friendly with elderly Mr Forbes, an adviser to the firm, who asks her to do him a favour by taking a parcel, containing a stamp album, to his sister-in-law, Agnes Turnbull, in Auchinleck, Scotland. But why does Agnes deny that she is the woman in question, and why does Helen find herself so attracted to Agnes's son, John?

MARY CUMMINS

A QUEST
SO STRANGE

Complete and Unabridged

LINFORD
Leicester

First published in Great Britain in 1972

First Linford Edition
published 2003

British Library CIP Data

Cummins, Mary
    A quest so strange.—Large print ed.—
    Linford romance library
    1. Love stories
    2. Large type books
    I. Title
    823.9'14 [F]

    ISBN 1–8439–5034–0

Published by
F. A. Thorpe (Publishing)
Anstey, Leicestershire

Set by Words & Graphics Ltd.
Anstey, Leicestershire
Printed and bound in Great Britain by
T. J. International Ltd., Padstow, Cornwall

This book is printed on acid-free paper

A Simple Request

As the long distance coach swung out of the Moor Lane Bus Station in the busy Lancashire town of Bolton, Helen Ferguson relaxed in her seat, hardly able to believe she was on her way back to Scotland.

She and her family had left Kilmarnock six months ago, and she had thought it would be many months before she would see Ayrshire again.

However, thanks to Mr Forbes, an older colleague, who had helped so much in settling her into her new job, she was using her two weeks' summer holiday to return to familiar ground, and try to carry out a very strange request.

A year ago the first hint had come of changes in the family circumstances.

Helen's father, Peter Ferguson, had had a good job with an engineering firm in Kilmarnock. But rumours had started that all was not well with the firm, and finally Mr Ferguson was made redundant.

At first he had high hopes of finding another job, but gradually his wife, Jean, who loved him dearly, had come to dread the look of disappointment on his face.

It was she who had urged him to look further afield.

'You wouldn't mind moving then, Jean?' he had asked her anxiously.

'Not a bit of it, so long as you found something suitable, my dear.' She looked at him fondly.

'But what about Helen? And Roger?'

'Helen's a trained typist. She can get a job anywhere. And Roger won't mind too much having to move to another school.'

Mr Ferguson's new job was in Bolton, and he travelled south a few weeks before his family to find a new home. Soon he was able to write to Jean, telling her it was all fixed up.

He had chosen a pretty house in Dunscar, and the family moved south to join him.

Surprisingly, it was Helen who found most difficulty in obtaining another job.

It was after her fourth interview that she started work in the offices of the large Langley Mills.

During her second month there, she first met Mr Forbes.

Miss Barlow, her supervisor, asked her to take a file along to the design office.

'It's for Mr Forbes, the elderly gentleman,' Miss Barlow told her. 'He's been with the firm forty-odd years, and is semi-retired. Sometimes he is called in to advise on special jobs, when his health permits.'

Helen had found Mr Forbes quite easily.

He had turned to her with a smile, when she approached his desk.

'Mr Forbes?'

'Yes, lass, that's me.'

'I'm Helen Ferguson. I'm new here. Miss Barlow asked me to bring you this file.'

As he thanked her, he scrutinised her carefully.

'Where are you from then, Miss Ferguson?'

'Kilmarnock, sir.'

'I thought it was somewhere like that. Have you ever heard of Tarbolton . . . or Tarbowten, as it was in my day?'

She grinned.

'Yes, sir. I know it well.'

He nodded a little, and she turned to leave.

'Have you settled in then, Miss Ferguson?'

She was taken aback by the question.

'Er . . . yes.'

The shrewd eyes twinkled, and Mr Forbes rose to his feet.

'If it's your coffee break now, we'll enjoy a cup together in the canteen.'

★   ★   ★

It was the start of a most rewarding friendship.

Helen often went to talk to Mr Forbes, especially when she was in doubt over her work.

Langley Mills had been a fairly small concern when he first started there, and he had watched it grow over the years. He knew all there was to know about the big concern.

Helen took the elderly man home to meet her parents, and they had spent a happy evening talking over places they had all known well.

Then one morning, only two weeks ago, she had gone to speak to Mr Forbes as usual. But, to her dismay, his chair was empty and his desk tidy.

'I'm afraid Mr Forbes is ill again,' another of the designers told her. 'His heart isn't good, and he often has long spells of rest.'

'Oh.' Helen felt her heart sink at the news.

'Have you got his home address?' she asked, slightly surprised to find that she, herself, did not know where Mr Forbes lived.

'I think so.'

He lifted up the telephone book, running his finger down a column.

'Here it is. Mr Gemmell Forbes . . . I'll write it down for you.'

That evening Helen put her coat on again after tea and looked for her piece of paper with Mr Forbes' address.

'It's in Astley Bridge,' she told her mother. 'I don't think that's far away. And I can soon ask.'

'Don't be late back, dear,' Mrs Ferguson told her. 'I don't like you to be out alone after dark.'

'All right, Mum.'

Helen found that the address in Astley Bridge was a charming small house, and a smart elderly lady opened the door.

'Mr . . . er . . . Mr Forbes, please?' Helen stammered, feeling quite ill at ease.

'He isn't very well, I'm afraid, Miss . . . ?'

'Ferguson. Helen Ferguson. I heard that he was unwell. I work in the office at Langley's. I've brought him some grapes.' She held out the parcel she was carrying.

The older woman's face relaxed in a smile.

'Ah, yes. Miss Ferguson. Mr Forbes has mentioned you. I'm Mrs Cameron, his housekeeper. Please come in, I'll find out if Mr Forbes can see you.'

★   ★   ★

Helen waited in the hall till the housekeeper came back for her and ushered her into the cosy bedroom.

She tried to hide her dismay when she saw how frail he looked, though he was obviously delighted to see her.

'I was just asking Mrs Cameron to try to get in touch with you,' he said, with satisfaction, 'only, I forgot your address.'

'I'm so glad I came then,' Helen replied warmly, taking a seat beside the bed. 'I've brought you some grapes, Mr Forbes.'

'That was kind. Let's have a few each, while Mrs Cameron gets us a cup of tea.'

After a while the old man asked her about holidays.

'They're in two weeks' time,' she told him. 'No-one in the office wanted theirs so early. As I'm new, I have to take them in June or in late September.'

'I see. Are you going away, Helen?'

'No, Mr Forbes. We're none of us having a holiday this year. My father likes his new job and doesn't want to take a holiday from it so soon. Anyway, we feel we've had enough expense with the flitting. I'm going to help Mother to decorate the kitchen instead.'

'I see.' The old man looked thoughtful as Mrs Cameron brought in the tea tray.

'Mr Forbes mustn't have more than one cup,' she warned Helen, 'so don't allow him to drink more.'

'She's far too bossy,' the old man said with a grin.

'I'll see that he sticks to one cup,' Helen told the concerned housekeeper, smiling.

After tea, Mr Forbes took up the conversation.

'There's something I want to ask you. It's very important and you're the only person I can trust. Would you consider going up to Auchinleck on an errand for me?'

'Auchinleck!' she repeated, rather taken aback.

'Yes. You see, I may have one relative still alive. A woman. She'll be about sixty or so, and I would expect that she's still alive. She was living in Auchinleck when I last knew her, and . . . and I want to give her something.'

'Oh!' Helen hardly knew what to say.

'Take a day to think about it. It's a fairly small parcel I'd like you to take. My stamp album, in fact. Agnes may have married, and have sons or even grandsons who would be interested in having it. I've always been a keen collector myself. Are you interested in stamp collecting, by any chance, Helen?'

'Not very much.' She laughed. 'Though my young brother is very keen.'

'Well, they've given me pleasure over many years, and I thought I'd hand them on to Agnes and her children, if she has any. As I say, it wouldn't be a big parcel, though Agnes may take a bit of finding. I thought you could speir aboot ... I mean, ask one or two people about her.'

'I'll speir aboot,' Helen replied, 'only ...'

'I would pay all your expenses, of course,' he broke in quickly, and the hot colour flooded her cheeks.

'Ask your mother and father first. And come back tomorrow night if you can go. I'll have the album ready for you then.'

'All right, Mr Forbes,' Helen told him.

As she rose to go, she bent on impulse and kissed his cheek.

★ ★ ★

Now, as the coach swung along through Chorley on the way towards Preston, Helen hugged the square neat parcel which she had agreed to try to deliver for Mr Forbes.

Her father and mother had been quite happy for her to undertake the errand, though she could not keep the worry out of her eyes when she thought about the man whose health made him look so much older than his age.

Helen had found a nurse in charge when she called the following evening, and saw that Mr Forbes looked weaker.

'They want to get me into hospital,' he told her gruffly. 'Maybe I will go. I don't want to be too much work for Mrs Cameron.'

'I'm sure she won't think of it that way,' Helen countered warmly.

'Have you thought about that

errand?' he asked. 'I'd like to have got in touch with Agnes Turnbull again, because of . . . well . . . everything that happened. She'll be my only living relative if she's still alive.'

'Is she your cousin?' asked Helen softly.

'No.'

There was a long pause, then the old man spoke gruffly.

'My sister-in-law. I . . . I married her sister over forty years ago, when we weren't much more than bairns ourselves. At least, she wasn't much older than a schoolgirl.'

'Oh,' Helen was taken aback. 'So you're a widower then, Mr Forbes?'

'Ay. I wasn't a husband long before I was a widower.'

Again there was a long silence.

'I found it hard to get work in Ayrshire after I left school,' he continued, 'and I came down to Bolton and got a start with Langley's. Edith and I had been meeting secretly. Her folks were grand people, if you know what I mean, and they had a big house in Auchinleck. I knew they would not want anything to do with a lad like me . . . without prospects. I felt I had it in me to make good in my job, and provide Edith with a good life once I got on my feet.

'As I say, we were only young at the time and very silly, with more dreams than sense in our heads. We got married secretly. We had the idea that Edith could stay on with her parents, if we said nothing, till I got a home for the two of us gathered together. She . . . she was a bit too delicate to rough it, and I was sure I could soon get established.

'But we couldn't keep in touch with one another. She would have had to explain my letters, and I was in and out of lodgings until I found a wee house for us. Six months after leaving I went home for her, only . . . '

Again Mr Forbes' voice trailed off.

'She had been knocked down by a car. In those days car owners were not always good drivers, and thought they should have the roads to themselves. Edith had been knocked down near her own gate, and taken to hospital . . . or so I was told.

'I managed to see her father, nearly forcing myself on to him, but I have never seen anyone who looked like he did. He said she was dead, and it was as though he had died a little himself. I . . . I never told him Edith was my wife. I felt I just couldn't claim her. I would have been trying to take her away from him all over again, and somehow it didn't seem to matter.

'But now I think I would like Agnes, her sister, to know the truth, that Edith had been my wife. She must have been knocked down before she could tell them, because Mr Turnbull looked on me as a complete stranger. We were only married six months,' he ended sadly.

'Oh, Mr Forbes,' Helen whispered softly. 'How sad for you.'

'It was a long while ago,' he told her, with a little smile. 'I learned to live my

14

own life by myself, and I've been fairly happy. It suited me at Langley's. Only . . . '

He reached over and picked up the stamp album.

'I like stamps,' he told her, 'that and gardening were my two main hobbies. I thought that if Agnes had married and had boys, they'd be men now. Maybe my stamp collection would come in useful.'

Helen took the album from his hand, seeing that it had been well used and loved.

'I tried to advertise for Agnes in all the papers, but it was no good. Now I'd like you to try. There's a letter with the album.'

'I'll do my best to find Miss Turnbull,' she assured him. 'My father will tie the album up in a parcel for me.'

'That's a good lass.'

He leaned back tiredly.

'If you don't find her, or if she has gone, then the stamp album is yours, Helen.'

'Oh, but surely . . . '

'No, I'm getting tired now. I've no more use for it, and if you don't fancy collecting any more stamps, then take it to Randle's. They'll give you a good price for it. I'll leave a letter to that effect. There's an envelope with money for the journey. Count it and see if there's enough.'

She counted.

'Mr Forbes! There's far too much!'

'Not a bit of it.' He smiled. 'If there's any left, buy yourself a fancy new hat, or whatever girls like these days.'

'It would buy dozens of hats. No, I shall bring it back to you,' Helen replied firmly, 'when I come to tell you how I got on with my search. You'd better tell me the address you knew years ago in Auchinleck.'

He gave it to her.

She wrote it down neatly in a small book, with all other particulars Gemmell Forbes could remember, including the date and place of his wedding to Edith.

It was early evening when Helen eventually left the coach at the busy bus station in Kilmarnock.

It was her mother who had suggested that she spend her first two days in Kilmarnock.

'Why not stay with Mrs McBride?' she'd suggested. 'She would be very pleased to put you up in her spare bedroom.'

Helen had coloured a little, turning away.

What about Alan McBride, she wondered?

The two families had been close friends as well as neighbours, and she had often had secret dreams that Alan would, one day, treat her as more than a young sister.

But when she had said goodbye before moving to Bolton, Alan had only given her a warm handshake, and his very best wishes that she and her family would be happy in Lancashire.

She had been too busy settling in and trying to find a job to let it bother her, but now she couldn't help wondering what her own reactions would be when she met Alan again.

At the bus station in Kilmarnock, Helen rose and tucked her parcel under one arm.

Her case was in the boot of the bus, and she followed the other passengers outside and round to the back.

Suddenly there was a hand on her arm, and she turned to find Alan McBride smiling at her.

'Hello, Helen. I thought you would be on this bus. I enquired at the booking office.'

'Alan! But there was no need. I mean . . . '

'Maybe there was no need, but I thought I'd like to come just the same. You look very well, Helen.'

He looked at her appreciatively.

She was wearing a smart navy blue suit, and a crisp white blouse, with navy shoes to match. Her glossy brown hair was neatly cut and combed to curl round her small head.

'Mum thinks you're bringing enough appetite for six. But don't worry. If you can't eat it all, I'll give you a good hand.'

'I expect you will,' laughed Helen as they made their way towards Alan's battered old car.

The moment she had been dreading had gone and it was just like old times between them. But Helen felt rather glad.

She was tired after her journey, and was beginning to feel the responsibility of her quest.

She kept seeing Mr Forbes' pale, tired face, and she was aware of how much the old man's friendship had come to mean to her. She must do her best to find Agnes Turnbull.

★　★　★

Mrs McBride was delighted to see Helen again. She had known the

Fergusons ever since Peter brought Jean, as a bride, to live in the good solid house two streets away.

And she had missed the Fergusons far more than she would have believed possible. It was a delight to have Helen to stay, even for a short time.

'My, this is a surprise!' she greeted the girl, hugging her. 'Can't you stay for your whole holiday? I couldn't quite follow why you've got to go to Auchinleck.'

'I'll tell you all about it when I get my breath back!' Helen laughed.

Over tea, she told the McBrides as much as she felt she could about Gemmell Forbes.

'He's been so ill that I feel I must do all I can to help him,' she ended, 'though the news was better the night before I came away. He was feeling quite a lot stronger.'

'He must have gone a bit queer,' Alan put in. 'Fancy expecting you to go knocking at a door and finding someone who lived there forty years ago!'

For probably the first time in her life, Helen felt a flash of annoyance at Alan.

'Of course he doesn't expect that,' she said rather sharply. 'I've just got to ask about, and see if anyone remembers the Turnbulls.'

'He should have kept in touch with his sister-in-law surely,' Alan persisted, and Helen bit back an angry reply.

She had felt it would be betraying a confidence to tell them the whole of Mr Forbes' story, and now she realised that Alan could not possibly understand.

Mrs McBride saw the annoyance in the girl's eyes and gave her son a warning look.

'Well, it's brought Helen back for an unexpected couple of days anyway. I'm very grateful to Mr Forbes, my dear,' she said hastily.

Helen felt a sudden lump in her throat. There was no doubt about her welcome back to Kilmarnock.

'Thank you,' she murmured.

'Tomorrow is Saturday, and my day off. Suppose we have a day out tomorrow, and a quiet day on Sunday,' Alan suggested. 'I'll run you up to Auchinleck on Sunday after tea, and find you suitable accommodation.'

'That will be fine,' Helen replied gratefully, her eyes shining again.

It would be wonderful to have a day out with Alan McBride. She saw admiration in his eyes when he looked at her, and felt her heart racing a little.

Maybe Alan had missed her a little. At least there was no doubt that he was pleased to see her back again.

On Saturday the weather warmed up and Helen was able to wear one of her pretty cotton dresses in pale pink and white candy stripes. When they met at the breakfast table, Alan said he had better give his car a quick wash down to make her a worthy vehicle for his passenger.

While he was splashing away in the yard at the back of the house, Mrs McBride turned to her visitor.

'You're settling down in Bolton then?' she asked with a smile.

'Oh, yes. Daddy loves his new job, so Mother was a long way to being happy when she saw him happy, too. Roger is at Bolton School and is doing well, and I like my new job very much.

'Mother is hoping you'll come and visit us for a few days. She thinks you would enjoy the change of shops and stores.'

'I would like that,' said Mrs McBride shyly. 'Maybe I could go later in the year.'

'We'll fix a date before I go home,' said Helen.

She rose to look for her short white coat and handbag as Alan appeared, ready to start the journey.

'Where shall we go?' he asked.

'Well, I've missed the sea,' Helen admitted. 'I've gone over to Blackpool with a crowd from the office once or twice, but it does seem further away now.'

'Right. We point the car towards the sea. Ayr might be busy today, but sometimes Troon is a bit quieter.'

It was a lovely day for both of them, but deep down Helen experienced one small disappointment.

She had always felt deeply attracted to Alan McBride, feeling that he was very different from any other young man she knew.

But six months had wrought a change, either in herself or Alan. She still liked him, and admired him more than any young man she knew, but the feeling that he was different from anyone else had gone. Now he was much more ordinary.

That evening on the way home, Alan kissed her for the first time, but Helen's heart wasn't deeply stirred.

'You . . . you like me a little, don't you, Helen?' Alan asked, and she nodded.

'I've always liked you, Alan.'

'It was only after you left that I realised I missed you a lot. I've been trying to write and tell you, but I'm a poor hand at letters. I couldn't make it come out on paper somehow. This holiday of yours was a splendid chance to talk to you. I thought I could tell you how I felt.'

She edged away a little.

'It's been a happy day, Alan. Something to remember when I go back.'

'It's been more than that for me. I think I'm in love with you, Helen, and I thought you cared for me.'

Helen tried to edge away from her companion. So Alan suspected her feelings for him, yet he had said nothing before she left Scotland.

She was glad of that, for she might have told him then that she loved him, when now she wasn't sure.

'I . . . I don't want to think about love, Alan. Not yet anyway.' Her voice was slow and deliberate. 'I like you better than anyone I know, but that's all I feel at the moment.'

She saw his disappointment.

'Have I been too slow then? Have

you met someone else?'

'Of course not.' She laughed.

'That's all right, then,' Alan said with relief. 'Look, Helen, we must keep in touch. Write to me sometimes and I'll try to write back. We mustn't let things slide between us.'

'All right. I'll write to you,' she promised. 'But I think we could only be friends, Alan.'

'That's good enough for now,' he told her happily.

So Frustrating . . .

Mrs McBride looked at Helen and Alan searchingly when they returned.

There was a momentary flash of disappointment in her eyes when she saw that they had no good news for her.

She would have loved to have Helen as a daughter-in-law, and had hoped that when the young people met again they would know how much they meant to one another.

She shrugged off her disappointment. It was a good sign that they were in no hurry. Quick, bright flames rarely make a glowing fire.

'How was Troon?' Mrs McBride asked, setting out mugs on a tray for their supper.

'Looking as beautiful as usual,' Helen assured her. 'We had a lovely day.'

'I hope there will be more lovely days to come.' Mrs McBride smiled, holding out the mug of coffee. 'Drink this. It grows chilly at nights here.'

'Thank you.' Helen accepted it gratefully.

It was chilly, somehow, yet it was still home. And it was nice to be back.

Helen wanted to find a private house in Auchinleck for the ten days which were left to her. She felt it would be less lonely if only she could find a nice 'Bed and Breakfast' place which would be willing to have her for longer than the one night.

She would be out most of the day, as her search might take her to nearby towns and villages.

She and Alan eventually found a very pretty cottage, well whitewashed, with pale blue paintwork and a neatly kept garden.

The woman who came to the door was plump, with smooth dark hair and a well-scrubbed look.

She seemed pleasant and motherly, and even Alan relaxed a little when she invited them both in to see a pretty lemon and white bedroom at the back of the house.

Helen found it an enchanting room.

'I'm afraid I would want it for a few days at least,' Helen told her hesitantly, 'Mrs . . . er . . . ?'

'Crawford. Lyn Crawford. It would be all right if you want to stay longer than a night. In fact, it would be fine. I won't have to change the bedding so often!'

Mrs Crawford smiled and looked at Alan, who was waiting quietly near the door.

'Mr McBride lives in Kilmarnock,' Helen explained. 'He has very kindly brought me to Auchinleck in his car. I'm Helen Ferguson and we used to be neighbours till my family moved.'

'What about your case then?' Alan asked.

'Oh, I'll need it out of the car,' Helen told him quickly. 'This will do fine, if the arrangement suits Mrs Crawford.'

'Will you be out all day then?' the older woman asked.

'Yes. Most probably. I'll see to my meals myself.'

'Well, I could manage an evening meal now and again. There's only myself and my husband, George,' Mrs Crawford explained. 'He works in a butcher's shop in town.'

'Fine,' said Helen, feeling thankful to be settled.

When she saw Alan off after thanking him, he bent and kissed her swiftly.

'Don't forget, if you get fed up with your task, or feel that it's just a waste of time, don't hang about here. Come on back to Kilmarnock.'

'All right, Alan.'

Helen smiled at him, touched by his concern.

'In any case, I'll come for you next Friday evening and you can stay overnight with us before travelling back home.'

'That will be splendid. Cheerio, Alan.'

She waved him away, her eyes sparkling a little with amusement, knowing that she had an audience in Mrs Crawford.

Smiling she turned back to the lovely little house.

That evening Helen went to bed early, in a hopeful frame of mind. She had met George Crawford, a large genial man with thin sandy-coloured hair and a smiling red-cheeked face.

Helen had explained very briefly that she had come to try to find the relatives of an old friend, who was too ill to come himself.

She asked directions to the address Mr Forbes had given her.

George Crawford had been very pleased to help, and had drawn her a nice clear map.

'Along there,' he said, marking off a street with an 'X'. 'That's where you want to go. A lot of folk from that area are customers of mine. Maybe I would know the person you want,' he went on helpfully. 'What name is it, please?'

'Turnbull,' Helen replied. 'Miss

Agnes Turnbull, though she may be married now.'

George's brows wrinkled, and he shook his head slowly.

'No, I can't say that rings a bell. Anyway, the neighbours will know. Somebody will be able to help you, I'm sure.'

'Good.' Helen sighed with relief. 'I'll be really delighted when I do find Miss Turnbull.'

★　★　★

The house, which had no doubt once belonged entirely to the Turnbulls, was split into flats. Four families lived there.

Helen stopped outside it, checking again that this was the correct address, then wondered which flat she should try first. She would need to try every one in turn.

Downstairs, to the left, she had to ring three times to make herself heard above the noise inside. Children were playing, and a radio blared out pop music.

Finally a harassed-looking young woman came to the door, and Helen rather haltingly asked if she knew about the people who had lived here before it was converted.

'They were called Turnbull,' she finished.

The young woman shook her head emphatically.

'We've only been here six months and we came from Cumnock before that. I'm sorry I can't help you.'

Helen was about to ask if she knew anything about the other householders, then she realised that the other girl had little time to spare. So she thanked her and rang the doorbell on the opposite side of the corridor. There was no reply, and the flat seemed silent and empty.

With a sigh, she climbed the stairs and tried the flat on the left of the landing. Again there was no reply.

As Helen rang for the third time, the landing door opposite opened. A woman with a round cheery face smiled out at her.

'If you want the McConnells, they both go out to work,' she was told. 'He has a hardware shop, and she helps him.'

'Oh, I do want them, but I'd like to speak to you, too,' Helen said with a smile.

'If you're selling anything, you've come to the wrong house,' the other woman told her with a rueful smile.

'No, I'm not selling anything, only trying to find some people.'

'Then you'd better come in,' she invited.

The flat was warm and cheerful, rather like its owner. Flora McGill, a widow, had lived in the house for the past five years.

'My son got married, so I gave them my house and came here,' she explained. 'I've been here longer than the McConnells and the Taylors downstairs, but not as long as old Mrs Mitchell. She's staying with her daughter this week, and won't be back till next Wednesday. I'm looking after her cat.'

Helen listened with interest while Mrs McGill boiled up a kettle and set out tea for both of them.

Obviously she was enjoying a bit of company, and was only too happy to talk to this attractive young stranger.

'Who did you say you were looking for?' she asked when they were settled.

'The Turnbulls,' Helen told her. 'Miss Agnes Turnbull, though she may be married now. I think they used to live in this house before it was divided up.'

'My, that would be a long time ago!'

'I'm afraid so,' Helen replied. 'I'd like to trace her for an old friend, who is rather ill. He knew the Turnbulls years ago. They're . . . relations.'

'Some folk are awfully casual about their relatives,' agreed Mrs McGill. 'They never bother with one another.'

'I suppose so,' interrupted Helen. 'If

you could remember anything . . . anything at all . . . I'd be very grateful, Mrs McGill.'

Mrs McGill did her best. She recalled every Turnbull she had ever known, but none of them answered the description given by Mr Forbes.

Helen was disappointed.

'Maybe I could try some of the other neighbours,' she said hopefully.

'Och, most of the houses are new round here,' Mrs McGill told her. 'No, your best bet would be old Mrs Mitchell, if you catch her on a good day. Sometimes her mind wanders a bit, but for the most part she can think pretty clearly.' She paused.

'You could try the McConnells, of course, but I doubt if you'll get much out of them,' she said frankly.

'I shall have to try everyone,' Helen assured her. 'Thank you for the tea, Mrs McGill. If you think of anything, I'm staying with Mr and Mrs Crawford . . . '

'Crawford, the butcher?'

'That's right.'

'Fine. I'll ask round about and see what I can find out. I hope you get the information you want all right. It's nice to see a young lass helping out an old man.'

* * *

That night Helen again climbed the stairs of the Turnbulls' old home, and this time she received a reply from the McConnells. 'I'm afraid I can't help you, Miss Ferguson,' Mrs McConnell told her. 'We've only been here for two years, and I don't remember anyone called Turnbull living here. How long ago did you say it was?'

'About forty years.'

Mrs McConnell tossed her head a little.

'Well, I could hardly be expected to remember that far back!'

'Oh, no, I am sorry,' said Helen, colouring. 'Of course I didn't mean did you know them personally. I only meant that you might have heard of the family.'

'I'm sorry.'

'Thank you,' said Helen, and went towards the door. She did not feel at all welcome in Mrs McConnell's charming flat.

Mrs McGill was dodging about on the landing, looking out for her.

'I saw you coming into the house from the window,' she said rather breathlessly. 'I bet you got no change out of the McConnells.'

'I didn't,' Helen agreed.

'Well, I've been asking about and I've got an address for you in Mauchline. My sister-in-law used to do some cleaning for folk in this road, before the houses came down. She used to know the housekeeper here. Only she can't remember the name of the folk. But the housekeeper lives in Mauchline, though she's an old woman now. She's called Mrs Beattie.'

Helen felt like hugging her.

'Thank you, Mrs McGill,' she said

sincerely. 'This will be a big help, I'm sure.'

'Glad to oblige,' the older woman told her. 'I hope you have a bit of luck in Mauchline.'

'I hope so too.'

Helen had not realised that trying to trace someone from years ago would be such a wearisome business.

'Come back and tell me how you get on, Miss Ferguson. We can have a wee bite of supper together,' Mrs McGill offered kindly.

'Oh, thank you,' said Helen again. 'I'll take the bus to Mauchline first thing in the morning.'

Mauchline had been bathed in a shower of rain when she arrived the following day. But the sun had now come out, making the flowers look fresh and beautiful, and the lovely old houses seemed so well cared for.

Helen remembered that the poet Burns had lived at Mossgiel Farm, near Mauchline, and could not help wondering if he had often walked on the very soil on which she now trod.

She paused to look at the slip of paper Mrs McGill had given her, with directions on how to find Mrs Beattie. The old housekeeper apparently lived with her daughter.

The house was small and neat, with a lovely garden. It was a middle-aged woman who opened the door.

★ ★ ★

'Mrs Beattie?' enquired Helen.

The woman didn't answer for a moment.

'No, I'm her daughter. Can I help you?'

'Well . . . '

Helen hesitated, wondering how to explain her errand.

'I'd like to talk to Mrs Beattie,' she said, after a moment. 'I believe she was housekeeper to some people I want to trace in Auchinleck.'

'Come in,' the woman invited.

The small sitting-room was perfectly

arranged, but it felt slightly cold and damp. Helen sat down rather gingerly on a lovely beige-coloured armchair.

'Er . . . ' she began.

'My mother is in the Eventide Home,' the other woman told her abruptly. 'She wasn't able to care for herself, and she wasn't happy living in with me and my family.'

Helen felt uncomfortable. She looked into the woman's face.

She could sense that there had been private trouble over this and felt that it was not her concern.

'If you would have no objection, I'd like to go and see her,' she said quietly. 'It's important to me to try and trace these people.'

'I'll write down the address for you.'

Helen smiled her thanks.

Somehow she was glad to leave the house with its new carpets and pretty curtains, walking down the street to find a café where she could have something hot to drink.

It was after lunch before she found

the Eventide Home, and met Mrs Beattie.

The woman who rose to greet her was tall and gaunt with sparse grey hair, but she looked strong and energetic.

'How did you know where to find me?' she asked sharply.

'Your daughter told me,' said Helen.

'Well, you can tell her I'm not coming back,' said Mrs Beattie roundly. 'I like my own kind of comfort . . .'

'I only came to ask about the Turnbulls from Auchinleck. They lived at 'Rowanlea' before it was made into flats. I understand you were their housekeeper.'

Mrs Beattie sat down.

'Turnbull, you say? That must have been before my time there as house-keeper. How long ago?'

Helen told her.

'Och, no, you've got the wrong folk,' said Mrs Beattie, nodding her head. 'I kept house for the Armstrongs till it was bought over and turned into flats. The Turnbulls lived there before the Armstrongs.'

'Did you know them?'

The old lady shook her head, and Helen felt her heart sink again.

She rose to her feet, and shyly took out a pretty box of chocolates from her bag.

'I'm sorry to have troubled you, Mrs Beattie,' she said quietly. 'I hope you won't mind accepting a small box of sweets.'

The older woman looked at the chocolates without speaking, then she looked at the young girl.

'You're a nice lass,' she said huskily. 'Nellie and Mamie and me . . . we all like chocolates. We'll enjoy these. Nobody bothers much nowadays. Miss Betty used to have young girls visiting her. Miss Betty Armstrong, that is . . . but I can mind no names at all.'

★ ★ ★

It had seemed rather a fruitless week, thought Helen the following weekend, when Alan McBride turned up unex-pectedly in his car.

He invited her to take a night off to go with him to the pictures in Kilmarnock. She was only too happy to oblige and felt delighted to see him again.

'My mother expects you for tea tomorrow,' he said firmly. 'Walking around trying to find someone is tiring work, and you're supposed to be on holiday as well.'

'I know,' Helen said ruefully. 'My feet do hurt a little.'

'Any luck?'

She shook her head.

She still felt this was a task she had to carry out, and she wasn't defeated yet.

She intended to interview Mrs Mitchell, even if the old woman's mind did wander sometimes.

Her daughter had been having her to stay for long spells, then she came back home for a week or two. She was due back on Wednesday, according to Mrs McGill.

However, the weekend proved a happy one.

Helen made arrangements with Mrs Crawford that she would stay in Kilmarnock until Monday morning, returning to Auchinleck for another few days.

During the weekend Alan wisely treated Helen like his good friend and companion. It was like a return of the past and they thoroughly enjoyed each other's company.

Alan, in his disappointment that Helen had been rather reserved with him, had confided in his mother. She had told him not to rush his fences.

Alan took her advice, and was realising more than ever how much he cared for Helen Ferguson.

'How is your friend, Mr Forbes?' Mrs McBride asked Helen. 'Is he any better?'

'Yes, thank goodness. When I rang home last night, Mother said she had been in touch with the nursing home.

He's making a very good recovery.'

She was silent for a moment.

If only she was going home with good news!

She realised that Gemmell Forbes was probably concerned to find himself some relatives — even relatives by marriage — now that he was growing older.

He had probably used the stamp album as an excuse to encourage her to look for Agnes Turnbull.

Yet it looked as though she was going to have little success, she thought despondently.

It was all a long time ago.

'Cheer up, Helen,' Alan was saying teasingly, though his eyes were serious. 'Care to go for a walk?'

'Yes, I'd like that,' she agreed. 'Just let me find my jacket.'

Mrs McBride watched them go from the window, seeing Alan draw Helen's hand under his arm. They were a fine young couple, she thought with satisfaction. She was glad Alan's heart was set on Helen.

And Helen? Well, she only needed time, thought the older woman comfortably.

She'd soon want to settle down.

Legal Advice

Helen called on Mrs McGill the following Wednesday before going to see old Mrs Mitchell.

Mrs McGill had been disappointed that her efforts to help the young girl had been fruitless, and now she was not very hopeful about the old lady.

'She manages very well in her own home,' she admitted, 'except, of course, that she forgets about things. Often she's as bright as a button.'

'Will you come with me, Mrs McGill?' Helen asked. 'Maybe a 'kent' face will be better than a complete stranger. I don't want to upset her in any way.'

Helen had bought a small gift of chocolates for Mrs Mitchell.

But when Flora McGill and she called in at the house downstairs, she found that her gift wasn't welcome.

'I never eat sweeties,' Mrs Mitchell told her. 'They're bad for my teeth. Eat them yourself, lass. They'd be lost on me.'

'Oh, well!' Helen was rather taken aback.

'The young lass wants to know if you remember the folk who used to live here,' Mrs McGill put in, speaking slowly and distinctly so the other would understand.

'Wait till I turn off the kettle,' the old woman advised, and shuffled through to the kitchen.

Helen had time to notice that the flat looked clean and fresh in spite of having an old-fashioned air, with biblical engravings on the wall, and dark green plush chairs.

Presently the old woman came back.

'Hello, Flora,' she greeted Mrs McGill. 'So you've dropped in to see me. Who's this?'

Helen's heart sank.

Mrs Mitchell had forgotten they were

there already! She would never be any help.

'We've just been telling you,' Mrs McGill said patiently. 'Do you remember the Turnbulls who lived here?'

Mrs Mitchell was gazing out of the window at the young children from next door who were playing hop-scotch.

'She had an accident, the wee lass,' she said sympathetically.

Helen sat forward.

'Do you mean Edith Turnbull?' she asked excitedly.

Flora McGill was shaking her head.

'I'm afraid she means wee Mandy Taylor from next door. She got knocked down by a van, but she wasn't badly hurt. In fact, now she can run and jump like the rest. That's her playing now.'

'It was a motor,' said Mrs Mitchell, clearly.

'That's right, a motor,' Mrs McGill said and whispered to Helen. 'I don't argue with her if I can help it.'

'Are you sure you don't mean Edith Turnbull?' asked Helen, though it now seemed a hopeless question.

Old Mrs Mitchell sat down suddenly.

'You stole my wee cheenie dug,' she accused Flora McGill.

'I only borrowed it,' Mrs McGill said soothingly. 'It's back on your shelf. See!'

'Oh, ay.'

Mrs Mitchell smiled at Helen.

'If you don't want the sweeties, I'll have them for the weans, lass,' she said gently. 'They like coming in for lemonade and a biscuit.'

'Here they are,' Helen offered.

'Thank you.' The old woman's eyes brightened. 'Have a good holiday. Flora will look after you.'

Mrs McGill rose.

'I'll bring you up to my flat for your dinner tomorrow,' she promised. 'Don't forget, Mrs Mitchell.'

'I won't forget,' the old woman told her cheerfully.

'She will, likely, and go starting to cook for herself,' Mrs McGill told Helen as they again climbed the stairs.

* * *

The young girl walked silently, feeling vaguely dissatisfied. She didn't feel at all sure that Mrs Mitchell had never known the Turnbulls.

She had a feeling that the old woman might have been able to tell her something if her mind had stayed clear.

Yet how could she badger Mrs Mitchell with questions?

She took her leave of Flora McGill, thanking her for all her kindness during her holiday.

The older woman had taken pleasure in arranging a lovely bunch of roses which the girl had brought.

'It's been a break for me, too.' She smiled pleasantly. 'I'm sorry you're going away, in fact.'

'I'm going to Kilmarnock tomorrow, then travelling to Bolton on Saturday,' Helen told her. 'It's been a bit tiring, but I've really enjoyed the holiday.'

'If you ever feel like another one,

come back and see me,' Mrs McGill invited.

She stood at the window a long time after the young girl had gone away, wondering if Helen would eventually be successful in her quest.

Helen enjoyed the journey south again, as she looked out at the slowly changing contours of the countryside.

The fresh green fields and sparkling white farms of Ayrshire gave way to rolling hills and fast-moving rivers of Dumfriesshire, then over the Border into Carlisle and the North of England.

It was late when she arrived home, glad to be welcomed once again by her family.

Over supper she had time for a second look at her mother, however, and began to notice that she looked rather pale and quiet.

'Is everything all right, Mum?' Helen asked anxiously.

Mrs Ferguson bit her lip and glanced at her husband.

'We wanted you to rest after your

journey before we told you,' she said slowly, 'but Gemmell Forbes had a relapse and died two days ago.'

'Oh, Mum!' The girl's eyes filled with tears.

'Yes, I know, dear. But he was an old man, and had been ailing for some time,' her mother said consolingly.

Helen sat quietly for a long moment.

'I . . . I'll miss him,' she murmured. 'He was very good to me, and helped me when I needed it most.'

'I know, dear,' her mother repeated.

'I'd better take the stamp album round to his house tomorrow, and the rest of the money from the holiday. I hardly needed even half of it. I expect Mrs Cameron will be there.'

She looked at her mother sadly.

'All right, Helen. Would you like me to come with you?'

But the young girl had grown more independent in recent weeks.

'No, it's all right, Mum. I'll go myself.'

Helen found Mrs Cameron looking slightly lost now that she had less work to do.

'I was so sorry when I heard the news,' Helen told her, 'especially when I couldn't find Mr Forbes' relatives. I tried as hard as I could, but it was just a hopeless task.'

'I think he expected that, my dear,' the older woman told her. 'Maybe he thought it worth a try, though.'

'Can you take the stamp album?' asked Helen. 'And this money that was left. He gave me far too much, really.'

'Oh, but you have to keep all that, dear,' Mrs Cameron protested. 'There's a letter here for you which he had witnessed. I know what's in it, though. He had few secrets from me. He's left me the house, you know, and a little bit of money. My husband was his best friend — he used to work at Langley's, too.'

'Oh, I didn't know.'

Helen was surprised at this piece of information.

'Yes. I've known Mr Forbes a long time. He said if you didn't find those people during your holiday, you were to keep the album. He suggested you sell it if you didn't care to collect stamps. Not everyone does.'

'I wouldn't dream of selling a gift,' Helen replied.

'Yes. I suppose he thought it was the best thing to do. Oh, and he said you must keep all that holiday money. He knew you'd try to give some of it back.'

Again Helen felt tears pricking her throat at the old man's generosity.

★　★　★

She stood up, hugging the stamp album which was still wrapped in a parcel.

'Are you staying on here, Mrs Cameron?'

'Yes, I have my own wee house across the road, but I think I'll let that. I've always liked this house best.'

56

'I'll come and see you sometimes.'

'Yes. Do that, dear.'

Helen went home slowly, her thoughts busy. It seemed as though a door had closed gently behind her. She would always remember Mr Forbes, but her own life stretched out before her. Already she could see alternative roads looming up.

Would she, one day, go back to Kilmarnock and Alan McBride? Or would some other way appear for her to follow?

With the passing of age, she felt her own youth, and the challenge of life ahead. Her step quickened as she reached her own avenue. Tomorrow seemed very inviting.

It was a warm summer.

In August Mrs McBride and Alan came down to stay and both families rejoiced in each other's company again.

The two older ladies loved browsing round the larger shops, or sitting in Victoria Square on the seats near the fountains, with the flowers in full bloom and the handsome Town Hall towering behind them.

Alan preferred to drive with Helen out to Rivington Pike or Winter Hill, where they could sit quietly in the car and look down on the large busy town with the hills beyond.

Helen, however, was equally good at keeping their friendship on the same basis as before.

She liked Alan better than any young man she knew, but she felt she didn't love him sufficiently for marriage.

'When is your next birthday?' Alan asked, the day before the holiday was due to end.

'December . . . just before Christmas,' she replied.

'I get holidays from the office at Christmas,' he told her. 'I want to discuss something with you, Helen. Something . . . well . . . important. But it can wait till then.'

She didn't pretend to misunderstand him.

'All right, Alan. We'll be pleased to

see you down again in Bolton.'

'In the meantime . . . '

He reached and pulled her into his arms, kissing her soundly.

'Don't, Alan!' she protested.

'I'm not rushing you, but don't think I'm slow either,' he warned.

'No,' she agreed. 'Only, one can't turn on love like a tap. Let's go back now, you've got a long drive ahead tomorrow.'

'All right,' he said, 'but don't go falling for any of your new acquaintances, that's all!'

★ ★ ★

In September, Roger went back to school, and the Fergusons felt that autumn was not so far ahead.

Helen was beginning to make new friends at Langley's, and she had joined a few local clubs.

'I used to think you should get out more,' her mother said, rather ruefully, 'but now I've got to keep you from

59

doing too much!'

'Oh, Mum!' laughed Helen. 'You're never satisfied.'

'Can I buy some more foreign stamps with my pocket money?' Roger asked. 'We've all got to take up extra cur . . . curricular activities,' he managed proudly. 'I'm taking up stamp collecting and Dad has given me his old books. Could I look at yours, Helen?'

She frowned a little. Roger was not always as careful with his possessions as he might be.

'You can look at it,' she said reluctantly, 'but no messing about with it. That album is precious to me.'

'I shan't mess about with it,' he told her with brotherly indignation.

It was quiet in the house that evening as the family pursued their various activities.

Helen was sewing a new blouse and her mother mending the lace on her pillowcases.

'Wow!' Roger said suddenly, as he pored over the stamp collection with his

60

magnifying glass.

'What's wrong?' asked his father, lowering his evening paper.

'It's this stamp in Helen's book ... the one she got from old Mr Forbes. It's valuable.'

'Well, you can't have it,' Helen said automatically, then asked after a pause, 'How valuable?'

'About a hundred pounds, it says in the catalogue,' was the reply from her awestruck brother.

'You and that old catalogue,' scoffed Helen. 'Your stamps are always worth a fortune!'

'No, but this one really is,' Roger insisted. 'Look, Dad, and see how carefully the stamp has been preserved.' He showed his father the stamp. 'And look at that one. Wow!'

'Don't keep saying that.'

Helen was beginning to feel half afraid of something, a feeling which she could not as yet define.

'Is it valuable, do you think, Dad?' she asked after a moment.

It seemed as though the whole family hung on her father's words as he looked closely at the stamp. After a while he raised his head and looked at Helen gravely.

'I think Roger's right, Helen. In fact, I rather think this whole album is valuable. Mind you, I'm not sure. But I think we ought to have it examined by an expert.'

'You'll come with me to have the album valued, Dad?' Helen asked.

'Of course, my dear. We'll meet somewhere at lunch-time tomorrow. I know a very good shop where they sell valuable stamps!'

'Randle's?' asked Helen. 'Mr Forbes said I could sell the album there.'

★   ★   ★

The following afternoon, Helen could hardly believe it had all happened. Almost in a dream she could hear the salesman congratulate her on a very fine collection.

When she mentioned Mr Forbes, his interest quickened . . .

'I thought I recognised some of these as his. Yes, Mr Forbes had as fine a collection as anyone I know.' He looked impressed. 'And he left it to you, Miss . . . ?'

'Ferguson.' Helen bit her lip, hardly knowing what to say.

'What valuation would you put on it?' asked her father bluntly.

'A conservative estimate? Oh, I should say . . . '

He mentioned a figure which made Helen blink.

'Should you wish to sell . . . ' he went on.

'There is no question of wishing to sell at the moment,' Mr Ferguson assured him. 'Come on, Helen.'

He took his daughter's arm and they left the shop together.

Helen turned large, rather frightened eyes to her father.

'And to think I carried it all the way up to Auchinleck and back,' she said. 'I

'. . . I could have lost it!'

'Not you. It had a different sort of value then, but just as precious to you, my dear.'

'Even more precious,' said Helen, ruefully. 'Oh, Dad! What do we do now?'

'Well, first of all I think we should see Mr Forbes' solicitors, just to make sure it should not go to someone else — Mrs Cameron, for instance,' he advised seriously.

'Then, if it's still yours, it will be up to you, my dear. If you feel you've got to go back and try all over again to find this Miss Turnbull, then you can go with my blessing. I'll do my best to help you financially for a few weeks.'

'I could manage quite well for a few weeks,' said Helen. 'After that I would just take things as they come. I'd better call on Mrs Cameron and get the name of the solicitor. Then we can take the album and the letter.'

'That will be best,' her father agreed.

The First Clue

It was two weeks later when Helen Ferguson again undertook the journey north, though this time it was quite a different journey from the last one.

This time she was clad in warmer clothing, had packed a larger suitcase, and was travelling north by train.

'I like going by coach,' she had protested to her mother.

'The summer service goes off soon,' Mrs Ferguson told her firmly, 'and it's too tiring by ordinary bus. No, if you go at all, you go by train. But I wish you would stay with the McBrides again, Helen. Won't they think it odd if you stay with a stranger?'

'Mrs McGill isn't really a stranger to me now, Mum,' Helen pointed out. 'She was very good to me when I was up last time and is delighted to have me. One could see that by her letter.

She has a nice spare bedroom, and I can be happy there.

'Besides, I have a feeling my only lead is old Mrs Mitchell, who lives in the flat below Mrs McGill. She's been in the district all her life and I feel she must surely remember the Turnbulls.'

Mrs Ferguson had sighed and given in.

Helen frowned a little now as she sat in the train. How could she explain to the McBrides that she wanted to be on her own?

She sighed.

Maybe in a day or two she would be glad to run to Alan and his mother. But at the moment, her life seemed to be a whole series of bridges which required to be crossed. That was just another of them.

Mrs McGill was delighted to see her again when she arrived at the small flat in Auchinleck.

'Come away ben, my dear,' she greeted Helen happily. 'This is the nicest surprise I've had for a long time.'

'Yes. I didn't think I'd be back so soon!' Helen laughed.

Flora McGill was as curious as the next woman, but she did not ask questions, contenting herself with seeing to it that her young guest was well fed and rested after her journey.

Helen, however, felt that Mrs McGill was due an explanation, if only in part.

'Mr Forbes died, I'm afraid,' she said regretfully. 'He left his relative a . . . well . . . a memento, so now I'm going to try to find her all over again. I didn't really work at it long enough before.'

'I thought you tried very thoroughly,' her new friend said stoutly. 'There aren't many young lassies who would have put themselves to so much trouble.'

'Well, I'm going to try again,' Helen told her.

She accepted another cup of tea.

'Er . . . is old Mrs Mitchell still downstairs?'

'Only until next weekend. Her

daughter has won the battle at last, and she's taking the old lady to stay with her. She's becoming so forgetful that they're worried she'll bring harm on herself.

'Why, Helen? Were you thinking of asking her more questions?'

The girl nodded.

'She's the only one who gave me something like a lead. Do you remember she said that a girl had been knocked down? Well, one of the Turnbull girls was knocked down . . . the sister of the woman I'm trying to find. She was killed by a car, poor girl. You see, Mrs Mitchell could have been talking about her, not about the little girl next door.'

Mrs McGill paused for thought.

'It's rather a thin hope,' she said, after a while, 'but I'll be having Mrs Mitchell up as usual for her dinner tomorrow.'

Next day, when Helen met the old lady again, it was obvious that Mrs Mitchell had completely forgotten having met her before.

'Did you say she was your niece, Flora?' she asked loudly. 'I didn't know you had a niece.'

'No, it's Miss Ferguson. You met her before when she came on holiday. She asked you about a family called Turnbull who used to live in this house.'

'Oh!'

Mrs Mitchell looked blank and Helen's heart sank again. There was no recognition at all in the old lady's eyes.

Instead she began to tell them about a young grandson who had made his mother a table at woodwork class in school.

'Guid as a table out of a furniture shop,' she said proudly. 'He's a clever wee lad.'

'Ay, they get well taught these days,' Mrs McGill put in.

'She was knocked down by a motor,' Mrs Mitchell said suddenly and clearly, while they were watching television.

'Who?'

'The Turnbull lass. She ran across the road and it hit her. They took her away to hospital but she never got better.'

Helen felt too surprised to speak.

'What about the other sister?' asked Flora gently. 'What was her name?'

'Agnes,' Helen interrupted.

'No, it's Karen, and she should have been Nancy, after me.'

Mrs McGill bit her lip.

'She's back at her grandchildren again,' she said to Helen.

For the rest of the old lady's visit, they had to be content to hear of a visit she once made to Edinburgh, then they both escorted her back downstairs to her flat.

'I know it's disappointing,' Mrs McGill said to Helen later, 'but her mind seems to work in flashes. Maybe she'll remember more now that we've set her on that track. Anyway, she'll be up for her tea tomorrow night. We'll play a game of dominoes. She's good at that.'

Helen could hardly wait for the

following evening, but she knew now that she needed great patience.

In any case, it was best just to enjoy the old woman's company without thinking of gaining any help from her.

★ ★ ★

Mrs Mitchell was surprisingly bright that evening, and was delighted when Flora brought out the dominoes after tea.

Helen laughed with amusement every time Mrs Mitchell couldn't play, when she would rap the table loudly and announce that she was 'chapping.'

'Segreave,' she said suddenly. 'It was a funny name and I knew it would stick in my mind. She married a Segreave.'

'Who?' breathed Helen, hanging on the old lady's words.

'The lass called Turnbull that Miss Armstrong knew.'

She wavered uncertainly for a moment. 'The Turnbull lass . . .'

'Agnes?'

71

'No . . . no, they didn't call her Agnes. It was . . . Betty. The lass married a Segreave from . . . '

Again she wavered.

'Where?' asked Mrs McGill urgently.

'Prestwick,' beamed Mrs Mitchell. 'I went there once.'

'To Prestwick?'

'No, to Edinburgh.'

Helen sighed a little, but she rose and dropped a kiss on the old lady's cheek.

It didn't look as though it was her Miss Turnbull, if she were called Betty, but at least she had somewhere else to investigate. Betty might even be a cousin.

'You're a good lass,' the old woman told her.

But was the information correct, wondered Helen.

Had a Miss Turnbull really married someone called Segreave and gone to live in Prestwick, or had old Mrs Mitchell once again become confused?

But it was a lead, and the only one she had got. That evening she talked things over with Mrs McGill.

'I think I'd better go to Prestwick for a few days, to try to check up,' she decided.

Flora McGill understood, even if she was loth to part with her young guest.

'Well, a neighbour of mine flitted to Prestwick two years ago. I'll give you her address. She'll maybe know where you can stay. You can always come back here, Helen, if you get tired . . . '

'Thank you,' Helen said gratefully. 'It's good to know I've got somewhere when home is so far away.'

'Ay, it will relieve your mother's mind, I'm sure, though I expect you've convinced her you can look after yourself.'

The girl laughed. 'Of course I have,' she agreed.

★ ★ ★

It was some years since Helen had visited Prestwick. Sometimes her family had enjoyed coming to the seaside on a warm summer's day, while young Roger had managed to coax them all in the direction of the airport, where he could watch the large planes taking off and landing.

Today was colder, however, and a fresh wind was blowing up from the sea.

But Helen felt oddly exhilarated as she walked down towards the sea front, eyeing the small neat houses until she found the address Flora McGill had written down for her.

She had already witten to her old friend and neighbour, and had received a reply, warmly welcoming Helen.

Mrs Cathcart was small and plump with short brown hair beginning to grow grey. She had a wide cheerful smile, and seemed delighted to see Helen.

'Why didn't Flora come with you?' she asked. 'I said in my letter I would like to see her.'

'She had already promised to see to

old Mrs Mitchell,' Helen told her regretfully.

'Yes, of course. Come on in, Miss Ferguson,' she said pleasantly. 'I've got the tea ready.'

Over tea Helen explained about her search, and asked Mrs Cathcart if she had ever heard the name Segreave.

'No, I don't think so. But then I haven't lived here all my life, and Prestwick is quite a big place now.'

'I'll just have to try and get digs for a few days,' Helen said, her eyes reflective. 'Do you know a boarding house nearby, Mrs Cathcart, or anyone who takes in boarders?'

The older woman regarded her thoughtfully for a moment.

'Well, today's Friday. So suppose you stay here till Monday. Then, if you have to stay longer, we'll see. I've got an extra room, but I've never thought of letting it.

'However, my husband is out all day whiles I feel I need more to do. I . . . I'd enjoy having you for the weekend, Miss

Ferguson. I know that if you get on with Flora, you'll get on with me.'

Relief showed in the younger woman's eyes.

'Oh, Mrs Cathcart, thank you very much. I couldn't wish for anywhere nicer. I hope I won't be a nuisance to you.' She smiled. 'And please call me Helen.'

'I'll be glad to have you, Helen.' Mrs Cathcart looked pleased. 'Can I pour you another cup of tea?'

Happily the girl handed over her cup.

'But how will you go about finding Mrs Segreave?' Mrs Cathcart asked. 'If it were me, I wouldn't know where to begin.'

'I could always begin with the telephone directory,' Helen explained. 'Then I think there should be a street directory giving the names of all the householders. Maybe I could find out at the Town Hall.'

'I've no telephone directory, I'm afraid,' Mrs Cathcart put in. 'I just go to the box on the corner.'

'Then I'll slip up there in a moment and look through the directory,' Helen replied. 'You never know, I might be lucky.'

Helen's hands trembled with excitement when she walked up the road to the telephone box at the corner.

★ ★ ★

There were two people in the book by the name of Segreave. She chose the first one, and dialled the number.

It was a woman who answered, and she said very pleasantly that she was Miss Segreave.

'I know this is an odd thing to ask,' Helen began, rather nervously, 'but I'm trying to trace a Miss Agnes Turnbull who may now be a relative of Mrs Segreave. Miss Turnbull came from Auchinleck.'

There was a short silence, then Miss Segreave laughed a little.

'How long ago would that be, Miss . . . er . . . ?'

'Ferguson. Helen Ferguson. It was about forty years ago, I'm afraid, Miss Segreave.'

'Not nearly long enough,' the other woman laughed softly. 'I'm over eighty, my dear. I'm afraid any relative of my mother would have been much too old for you.'

'I'm sorry.' Helen felt the colour rise in her cheeks.

'I can't help you, my dear. I've got no relatives at all now. I'm so sorry.'

Helen put back the telephone, then looked at the next name — John Segreave — hesitating even more.

She wasn't really enjoying this task. But each day that passed only strengthened her resolution to find the real owner of Mr Forbes' stamp album.

Now she bit her lip and picked up the telephone again. This time there was no reply.

Helen allowed it to ring for a time, but it was obvious that there was no-one to answer it.

She pulled out a piece of paper from

her handbag and carefully copied down the address.

Tomorrow she would call on the people there, and this time she hoped for more success.

★   ★   ★

It was Sunday afternoon before Helen was successful in finding anyone at home at the Segreaves' address. By that time she was beginning to feel rather depressed about her quest.

For one thing, her money was beginning to run out. She had budgeted carefully, but even so, it was difficult to live within her means and she wanted to manage on her own.

She began to wonder what she ought to do if she received no response from the Segreaves. Perhaps they were away from home, and would not be back for a week or two.

If so, she would want to stay on in Prestwick. It occurred to her that she might try to find a job.

Her thoughts were still busy with this idea when she rang the doorbell of the charming solid-looking detached house at the address she had taken from the telephone directory.

A few minutes later the door opened and a young man with unruly dark hair stood there, a slightly harassed air about him.

'Yes?' he asked. 'What can I do for you?'

'My name is Helen Ferguson. Are you Mr Segreave?'

The young man nodded and smiled briefly.

'John Segreave . . . '

'I . . . I wonder if you can help me,' Helen asked nervously. If only John Segreave knew something the past weeks would seem worth while. 'I'm trying to trace a Miss Turnbull who used to live in Auchinleck. I understand that a lady called Turnbull married a Mr Segreave. I've been hoping she was a relative . . . '

'Please come in.'

Mr Segreave held the door open, and led the way into a pleasant room at the back of the house.

'Look,' he said, again looking rather harassed. 'I've got to see to something in the kitchen. I'm looking after myself for a week or two . . . '

'Can I help?' asked Helen, but he'd already disappeared through another door leading from the hall.

She could smell something burning, as though milk had boiled over on the stove.

She hesitated for a moment, feeling too shy to push her way into the kitchen.

Yet it seemed to her that young Mr Segreave seemed to be in need of help.

While she was making up her mind, he returned, his pleasant smile rather crooked.

'I'm not at my best in the kitchen, I'm afraid.'

'Can I help?' she asked again.

'Well, perhaps in a moment. We'd best find out if I can help you first of

81

all, though. You want a Miss Turnbull who lived in Auchinleck?'

'She was born in Auchinleck. The family moved away when she was in her teens. Her name was Agnes, but I understand your mother's name was Betty.'

'I'm afraid not,' John Segreave replied. 'I'm an orphan. My mother was Irish and she died when I was born. My grandmother brought me up for a while, then I came to live in Ayr with my father. I was fourteen when he died, so my aunt and uncle gave me a home. Maybe you want my Aunt Nan.'

Helen's heart leapt.

Nan! Wasn't that short for Agnes?

'Was she called Turnbull?'

'Yes, she was. But she certainly doesn't belong to Auchinleck. As far as I know, she had no connection with it at all. She lived in Moffat before she was married, and still speaks with an accent. I wouldn't be sure she's the one you want.'

'She sounds the most hopeful person

I've heard about,' Helen replied. 'Maybe the family moved to Moffat some time ago.'

'I can only say that she's never mentioned Auchinleck to me.' He eyed her questioningly. 'Anyway, you haven't told me why you want her.'

'Oh, sorry.' Helen blushed a little.

* * *

She was beginning to find this tall young man with the unruly strands of curling black hair rather disconcerting.

'I've got something for her from an elderly gentleman who was a friend of mine. He was Mr Gemmell Forbes and . . . '

'Was?'

'I'm afraid so. He's dead now, but he's left a stamp album to Miss Agnes Turnbull whom he knew years ago.'

Helen stopped, biting her lip. If John Segreave's aunt was the Agnes Turnbull she wanted, then it would surely be all right to tell him the story.

But if she wasn't, then perhaps she ought not to explain very much more at this stage.

John Segreave's eyes were full of interest and surprise.

'What an odd thing to do!'

'It might seem so at first, but he really treasured his stamps.'

The smile left the young man's lips and he nodded soberly.

'I know what you mean. I don't collect stamps myself, but I do buy books, and I treasure those. If I ever gave them to anybody, then it would have to be someone I really cared about.'

Helen nodded, pleased that he understood.

'Could I possibly see your aunt, Mr Segreave?' she asked, a trifle breathlessly. 'I've been looking for Miss Turnbull for ... well ... weeks. It would be really wonderful if I've found her at last.'

'She's away on a business trip with my Uncle William,' John Segreave replied regretfully. 'They'll be away for about three weeks yet, I'm afraid.'

'Oh!' Helen was almost sick with disappointment.

Now she really would have to try and get a job, if she must stay in Prestwick for three weeks.

'I'll just have to come back then,' she said, rising to her feet.

'If you leave me your address, I'll let Aunt Nan know you've called. Do you live locally, Miss Ferguson?'

She shook her head.

'I live in Lancashire now. I'm only staying in Prestwick temporarily.'

She wrote down Mrs Cathcart's address.

'You'll be staying on here then?' he enquired.

'I'm afraid so. I can't go home without trying to see Mrs Segreave and finding out if she's the Miss Agnes Turnbull whom Mr Forbes knew, or if old Mrs Mitchell has confused her with someone else. It could easily have been another Agnes Turnbull who was friendly with the Armstrongs.

'Mrs Mitchell . . . ' Helen smiled indulgently. 'She tends to get a little bit confused now.'

'She's not the only one.' John Segreave grinned ruefully as a smell of burning again wafted from the kitchen. 'I have a woman coming in to help during the week, but I manage for myself at the weekend.'

'Then you must allow me to help you a little today,' Helen offered, with a friendly smile.

John Segreave's brown eyes became warm with gratitude as they rested on her.

'To tell the truth, I'd welcome a meal that tastes of something else other than cinders.' He grinned. 'How about us having a cup of tea and a sandwich?'

Helen left the house just over an hour later, having restored order to the kitchen, and served up a quick omelette for John.

She only accepted a cup of tea and a biscuit for herself, and over tea she told him as much as she could about her search for the owner of the stamp album.

'Haven't you even heard your aunt talking about a sister, Edith?' she asked hopefully.

John shook his head.

'Never, I'm afraid.'

'I'll have to get a temporary job,' she told him, watching with pleasure while he tucked into the light, fluffy omelette.

He looked at her reflectively.

'What do you do?'

'Oh, office work, mainly. I can type and do shorthand.'

'If it's only a temporary job, I believe you could get in at the airport in one of the freight offices. Permanent jobs there are much more difficult to get. Sometimes staff are sent up from London, and there are always lots of people looking for openings.

'But, if you're interested, I could write down the particulars for you, and you can try there.'

'That would be splendid,' said Helen

happily, and watched while he wrote it down for her on a card.

It was only later that she wondered how he came to know about such a job.

Did he work there himself?

In spite of the anti-climax in finding that Mrs Segreave would be away for three weeks, it had been an exciting afternoon, and Helen carried the memory of a pair of dark brown eyes, earnestly looking into her own.

There was something about John Segreave which made him different from any other man she had ever met.

Suddenly Shy

Helen Ferguson lost no time in applying for the secretarial post at the airport.

Three days later, dressed carefully in her smartest suit, she made her way to the airport building for an interview.

Although she felt rather nervous, she proved herself to be competent, and an hour later she was able to look forward to starting work there the following Monday.

It promised to be an exciting job.

Helen was fascinated by the main airport building, looking with interest at the smart ground hostesses in their becoming uniforms of the various airlines.

The continuous flow of people arriving and departing from the airport bewildered her, but she would get used to it in time.

Her thoughts went back to John Segreave, as she left the building. She would ring up and thank him, she decided, then remembered he would probably be busy at his own job at the moment.

She would have to phone in the evening.

Mrs Cathcart was delighted with Helen's news when she returned to the little house near the seafront.

The girl had settled in very well, and it had been decided that she should stay there, on very reasonable terms, for as long as was necessary.

'I'll have to write and tell my parents and, of course, Mrs McGill,' Helen told her kindly landlady. 'They were expecting me home.'

'Your mother must be missing you,' Mrs Cathcart remarked, and some of the light died out of Helen's eyes.

She missed her family quite a lot, too, now that her absence from home had been prolonged.

It was the first time she had been

away from her family, and sometimes she felt rather lonely and cut off.

'Perhaps it's good for me to have to stand on my own feet,' she reflected.

'Of course, my dear. When you write to Flora McGill tell her that I could do with a visit from her.'

'Of course,' Helen agreed. 'It will be nice to see Mrs McGill again.'

'And . . . you've still no notion whether you've found the lady you're looking for?' Mrs Cathcart asked diffidently.

Helen shook her head.

'I'll have to wait till she gets back to Prestwick,' she said, with a small sigh. 'It could be the same Agnes Turnbull, but her nephew doesn't think she ever lived in Auchinleck. He says she's from Moffat.'

'Well, I suppose it's a common enough name,' said Mrs Cathcart. 'There must be a few Agnes Turnbulls around, but not many married to someone called Segreave.'

'No, but old Mrs Mitchell could have

mixed up my Agnes Turnbull with another one. She gets so confused.'

'Anyway, it's giving you the opportunity of a new job at Prestwick. I'm sure you'll enjoy that.'

'I'm sure I shall, too. And I must thank Mr Seagreave because I understand jobs aren't so easy to get.'

Helen coloured a little, and felt the blush deepen as Mrs Cathcart looked at her curiously. She had secretly hoped that John Segreave would get in touch with her again, but there had been no word at all. But there was no harm in hoping . . .

That evening, after she had posted her letters, Helen went to the telephone box and rang the Segreaves' number. But there was still no reply.

Disappointed, she left the call box despondently, and made her way back to Mrs Cathcart's, where she penned a polite little letter of thanks, and went out to post it.

No doubt she would hear again from Mr Segreave in about three weeks' time, if he kept his promise, letting her know if she could come and talk to his aunt.

Meantime she had her job to look forward to.

She took a walk down to the seafront and looked out at the grey sea, the waves frilled with foam.

The Arran coastline was shrouded in mist, and Helen shivered a little, pulling the collar of her coat up round her neck. The warm summer days were over for this year, she decided.

The girl swung along the quiet streets which had been so busy with holiday-makers a few weeks before. She felt oddly reluctant to go home, telling herself it was because of the attractive job which was now hers.

Yet deep down she knew it might be because of a desire to see John Segreave again.

But she wouldn't admit to that.

Quickening her step, she hurried back to Mrs Cathcart's, where a hot drink was waiting for her.

The warm fire and the hot milk made her sleepy, and she went off to bed.

★   ★   ★

At the weekend Helen had a letter from her mother, full of news about the family, and congratulating her on her new job.

So long as you're happy in Prestwick, Helen, she wrote, *we're happy for you to stay there.*

By the way, I had a letter from Mrs McBride. She was very surprised to hear you are back in Scotland. I think Alan is a little hurt that he hasn't heard from you . . .

Helen read the letter, flushing guiltily.

She had spared a thought now and again for Alan McBride, but she had shied off going to see him.

She did not want to have to think too much about her feelings for Alan while she had another problem to solve.

Now she realised that her mother was

probably hinting that she had been wrong in not going to see them.

Both Mrs McBride and Alan had been kind to her in the past, and this was no way to repay that kindness.

'I would like to go to Kilmarnock today,' she told Mrs Cathcart on Saturday morning. 'I have friends there I wish to see.'

'All right, dear,' the older woman replied. 'Does that mean you'll be out for lunch?'

Helen nodded, her mind busy with plans.

If the McBrides were out, she would spend the day wandering round the Kilmarnock shops.

Helen dressed carefully and bought some flowers for Mrs McBride.

When she reached their home in Kilmarnock, she couldn't help colouring a little when the door opened and Alan stood there.

'So you've decided to visit us at last,' he said flatly.

'Oh, Alan, I'm sorry. I know I should

have let you know I'm in Prestwick, but somehow . . . '

She bit her lip as Mrs McBride came forward.

'Well, you're welcome now you're here,' the older woman said warmly. 'Take her coat, and poke up the fire, Alan.' She smiled to Helen. 'Your mother said you are staying for a few weeks.'

'Yes, I've got a job at the airport starting on Monday,' she told them.

'That's splendid.' Mrs McBride glanced at her son, then excused herself, saying she would just see to the lunch.

'I hope I haven't upset your arrangements,' Helen said, as Mrs McBride was opening the door.

'Of course not. I always cook more than we need. You know that, dear.'

A moment later Helen and Alan were left alone in the living-room.

'You've been hiding from me, haven't you?' Alan muttered accusingly and Helen knew that what he said was true.

'Well, perhaps you're right, Alan. Maybe I was. You said we could talk about things in December. Well . . . I don't want to think about my own future before then, that's all.'

'And you think I'm the sort of chap who keeps on at you when you don't want to be bothered?' he asked huffily.

'No, of course I don't.'

Helen's cheeks coloured again.

'Well, you can stop worrying,' he told her crossly. 'I won't bother you.'

There was a heavy silence between them when Mrs McBride came back to say that lunch was ready, and she looked from one to the other.

It was rather a silent meal, and after Helen had helped with the washing up, she excused herself, saying she had to get back to Prestwick.

Her visit hadn't exactly been a success . . .

★   ★   ★

'I'll see you on to the bus.' Alan told her, and would listen to no arguments.

As they strode along side by side, Alan suddenly caught her arm and led her down a quiet lane.

'I'm sorry, Helen,' he began. 'I was hurt and angry, knowing you were nearby yet avoiding me. But I realise now it's my own fault. I still want to talk to you in December, but meantime I shan't see much of you if you don't want it. Will that do?'

She felt tears catch in her throat.

'Oh, Alan,' she said. 'You're such a good friend. I should know what I feel about you now, only . . . '

The vision of a thin brown face with crisply curling dark hair kept intruding on her thoughts.

Surely she could never fall in love with Alan if she found another man so attractive, even if he was almost a stranger to her.

Helen pulled herself together.

John Segreave was a stranger, and because of that she must be imagining the attraction she felt.

It was made up of dreams, not reality.

'There is still no-one else?' Alan asked anxiously, watching her expressive face.

'I . . . no, of course not.'

Alan held her arm a moment longer, standing very still, then he grinned and kissed her lightly on the cheek.

'Airline pilots are unfair competition,' he told her lightly. 'Remember that. They've got plenty of girls falling over them already without you.'

She laughed, matching his mood.

'I thought you had, too, Alan.'

'I can pick and choose,' he told her modestly. 'Aren't you flattered I've chosen you?'

Her eyes danced. This was more like the Alan she knew.

'Very flattered.'

But as he waved her away on the bus, Alan's smile turned to a scowl. Never before had his friendship with Helen meant so much, and it looked as though there might be some competition.

She had said very little about her search for the woman she wanted to trace, other than that she might be a lady at present away with her husband.

'Is there any family?' Mrs McBride had asked.

'No. Only a nephew.'

Alan's eyes grew thoughtful as he strode home. Was it that nephew who had caught Helen's interest, or someone she had met at Prestwick?

*   *   *

Helen felt rather strange on her first morning in her new office at the airport, but towards lunch break one of the other girls came up to her desk and offered to show her the canteen.

'I'm Moira Bryden.' She smiled warmly. 'It isn't so long since I was new here, and I know how bewildering it feels. I thought you'd maybe like to go with me.'

'Oh, thank you. I'd appreciate that very much.'

As they walked through the large main building, Moira smiled pleasantly to other members of the staff.

'Those girls are ground hostesses,' she explained.

'They look very smart,' Helen said shyly, eyeing one particularly lovely girl. 'Are they attached to their own particular airline?'

'That's right. They meet people coming in, and help passengers through Immigration . . . that sort of thing.'

'It sounds awfully interesting,' Helen remarked, as she followed Moira into the canteen.

After lunch, they went on a tour of the building. Moira pointed out the airline offices, the rest room and shops.

'I see the luggage is put on a sort of conveyor belt,' Helen said.

'A 'carousel'.' Moira smiled. 'It's been known to break down, too.'

'What's that?' Helen pointed to another object.

'Oh, that thing tests for potential hi-jackers.' The smile died out of her eyes. 'It's sad that it's necessary to have such a thing.'

Helen nodded soberly, and asked if they could look out at the runway, where the large planes stood waiting to be loaded up before departure.

'Do you ever long to fly off somewhere instead of going back to the office?' Helen asked laughingly, as both girls turned away.

'Sometimes, on a very nice day. The feeling doesn't last long, though. I don't think I'm very adventurous. Are you?'

Helen considered.

'No, I don't suppose I am. Not really,' she conceded, then started a little as she caught sight of a tall man with curling dark hair disappearing in the direction of the airline offices.

Her heart raced and she felt her cheeks grow warm.

'What's the matter? Have you spotted a celebrity or something?' Moira asked teasingly.

'No. I ... I just thought I saw someone I knew,' was Helen's hasty reply.

The glimpse had been so fleeting that she decided she must be imagining things.

It wouldn't do to keep thinking she was seeing John Segreave round every corner!

'Back to work then,' said Moira. 'Do you live in Prestwick, by the way, Helen?'

'Only in lodgings. My parents live in Lancashire.'

She was about to ask Moira more about herself, but it was time to tackle the work which was piling up.

She was getting used to this, and knew that she was capable of dealing with it. The knowledge gave her a warm glow of satisfaction, and she felt happy in her new job.

That afternoon, as Helen left the office along with Moira, she felt tired but oddly satisfied.

'I've enjoyed today,' she told her new friend.

'That's good. Have an early night all the same. Anything new like this can be a bit of a strain.'

'Don't worry. I will. I . . . ' She broke off again, her eyes on a tall figure walking ahead of her.

Surely it was John Segreave . . .

'What's wrong?' asked Moira.

'It's just someone I've seen. I thought I knew him . . . the tall man ahead.'

'Mr Segreave? He's the manager for Albatross Airlines. You were admiring one of their ground hostesses today. The tall, fair girl in the cream-coloured uniform. She's Annette Thompson. There she is, talking to him now.'

Helen's cheeks had flushed crimson.

'Are they friends?' she asked.

'Special friends, do you mean?'

Helen nodded.

'I rather think so, though I don't really know.' Moira looked at her more closely, wanting to ask if it mattered, but feeling it was none of her business.

'Do you know Mr Segreave?' she asked, after a while.

'I've only met him once. He recommended me to try for this job, but I didn't know he worked here.'

'I see.'

As they parted Moira smiled cheerfully at Helen.

'Don't forget . . . an early night, and I'll see you again tomorrow.'

'Goodnight, Moira.'

Helen was very thoughtful as she went back to Mrs Cathcart's. She could see now why she hadn't heard from John Segreave again. He had probably forgotten all about her.

But even that glimpse of him had been enough to stir up her own interest, and Helen had to take herself severely to task.

She couldn't possibly be attracted to someone she didn't know, someone who was obviously already interested in a much lovelier girl, if what Moira had said was true.

★ ★ ★

On Friday evening there were two letters waiting for Helen when she got home.

'The post was late this morning,' Mrs Cathcart explained. 'They came just after you left for work.'

One was from her mother, a nice newsy letter from home.

Helen picked up the other and glanced at the bold handwriting curiously, then opened it.

It was from John Segreave.

I have now been in touch with Aunt Nan, he wrote, *having spoken to her on the telephone. I'm afraid she isn't the lady you wish to meet.*

She says she never knew anyone called Mr Gemmell Forbes, and has no relatives who can help you.

However, I had an idea myself, and I wonder if we could meet for a meal tomorrow evening, I'll tell you about it then. May I call for you at about seven-thirty? Ring if it isn't convenient.

Helen read the letter again, torn between disappointment and happiness.

Only now did she acknowledge to herself how much she'd wanted Mrs Segreave to be her Agnes Turnbull.

It would have given her a great deal of pleasure to hand over the valuable stamp album to John Segreave's aunt.

But now she realised that she had pinned too many hopes on the information given to her by a confused old lady.

Yet, what further lead could Mr Segreave have?

Helen's first instinct had been to refuse the invitation after she thought about it for a little.

She had been beginning to laugh at herself for being so attracted to a stranger, and to concentrate on her new job instead.

Suppose she got to know John Segreave better, and the attraction deepened . . . what then?

She would only be hurt by it all.

Helen bit her lip.

Surely, it was necessary for her to explore every avenue to find the true owner of Mr Forbes' album.

If she didn't make more progress, she might as well go home.

For her date with John Segreave, Helen wore a new tweed coat and dress in misty blue. She had brushed her soft brown hair till it hung in a cloud round her face.

When John Segreave arrived, Helen greeted him shyly and rather awkwardly.

He looked somehow older and more reserved than the cheerful, rather untidy young man she had met a week or two ago.

Or could it be that she now looked on him differently, knowing his position at the airport?

'I thought we might drive along the coast,' he suggested, helping her into the car. 'I know somewhere nice in Troon, if that would do.' He looked at her with a smile.

Helen only hesitated for a moment, remembering the day she had spent there with Alan.

'That would do fine. Thank you for inviting me,' she said, with a quick shy answering smile.

For a while there was silence between them as John drove the short journey to Troon.

He stopped in the car park of an attractive hotel. Then he turned to Helen, his eyes questioning.

'What's wrong, Helen?' he asked bluntly.

'Wrong? Why . . . nothing,' she stammered, blushingly. 'What could be wrong?'

'You seem different somehow, as though you've become suddenly wary of me. Do you mistrust me over asking Aunt Nan questions and think I'm putting you off?'

'Oh no, it isn't that,' Helen cried quickly.

'Then there is something?'

'Only that I got the job at the airport, Mr Segreave.'

'Congratulations.'

'But I didn't know you worked there

and are, in fact, one of the airline managers.'

'What has that got to do with it?'

'I've been used to office etiquette at Langley's. We weren't encouraged to be friendly with managers of other departments.'

John pursed his lips.

'I don't see that applies. You're only here temporarily after all. But if it worries you, then we can be friends out of office hours, in our own time and you can call me John . . . Would you prefer that?'

He met her gaze earnestly.

'I did think we were going to be friends, Helen. I also thought it would be nice if you worked nearby, then you won't be rushing off home before you've found the lady you're looking for.'

'I shan't do that,' she said quickly.

'No, of course you won't. I'd like to help you, if I may.'

Helen smiled.

'Thank you, John. I'd appreciate any

help you can give me, and I would like to be friends out of office hours.'

'Come on then. Let's have our meal before I die of starvation!'

* * *

It wasn't until after their meal, when they relaxed over coffee, that John again brought up the subject of his Aunt Nan.

'I think I'll have to wait till they come home before I talk to her,' he confided to Helen. 'She hates having long conversations on the telephone.'

'But if she isn't my Agnes Turnbull, how can she help?' Helen asked.

'Well, it seemed to me the common link was Betty Armstrong. She was Aunt Nan's bridesmaid, and if old Mrs Mitchell was right, she also knew your Agnes Turnbull . . . '

'You mean she would know two Agnes Turnbulls?'

'Why not? I know three Bill McIntyres. It's not such an unusual name.'

'No, I suppose not. But how do I find

111

Miss Armstrong? She might be as hard to find as my Miss Turnbull.'

'I'll find out about her from Aunt Nan, when she gets home. I can't get her to talk about personal matters on the telephone. She thinks it's a waste of good money unless we confine our conversation to whether I'm well or not, and if I'm having enough to eat.'

Helen laughed. She had relaxed in John's company and was completely happy.

'Even if it's a dead end, I hope you'll stay on for a week or two, Helen,' he said suddenly. 'You look more carefree than you did when I saw you before. Are you enjoying it all?'

'Yes, I am,' she said frankly. 'I've met a new friend called Moira Bryden . . . '

'I know Miss Bryden.'

'And Mrs Cathcart spoils me. I suppose I like being near my old home for a little while at least, too.'

'Perhaps we could go to the pictures some time. Or do you like dancing?'

She laughed.

'I don't go dancing very much, but I like a good film or concert when I can manage to go.'

'Fine. I'll call for you again next Saturday, if that's all right.'

There was a pause while he paid for their meal.

'Oh, no, it will have to be the following Saturday, I'm afraid,' he corrected. 'Is that all right?'

'That will be fine,' said Helen, her eyes shining.

It was a cool evening when they returned to the car park, and Helen shivered a little when John helped her into the car.

'Here, we mustn't have you catching cold,' he told her, tucking a car rug round her knees.

She relaxed, feeling pleasure in being looked after for a little while.

It was as they drove away from the car park that Helen caught a glimpse of someone staring at them for a moment from another car, and the face teased her memory. It was that of a lovely girl with long loose-swinging blonde hair.

Much later Helen realised that the girl looked like Annette Thompson, whose hair was normally caught up in neat rolls under her smart little hat.

Near To Tears

Helen began to settle into a happy routine for her new job. She didn't expect to be at the airport for more than a few weeks, so she decided to make the most of her time there.

She met John Segreave occasionally in the course of her work, and they greeted each other pleasantly. But she didn't mention her friendship with him to anyone, not even Moira.

A day or two after their dinner date she was glad about that, for she overheard a remark made by Annette Thompson.

The other girl had been looking at Helen curiously every time they met in the canteen.

Helen, remembering the girl they'd seen on that date, began to feel convinced it had been Annette in the other car at Troon.

While she and Moira were enjoying a cup of coffee one afternoon Annette and a friend came to sit at a nearby table in the canteen.

Helen couldn't help overhearing their conversation, as the canteen was quiet.

'I thought my pale green midi-length dress would be nice,' Annette was saying. 'And I'll wear my hair down again. It's a very special affair. There's to be a dinner followed by a dance . . . '

'You should look wonderful, Annette,' her friend told her warmly.

'Well, Daddy is one of the organisers, and John is going as my partner . . . '

Helen felt her cheeks going warm, unwilling to hear more, but finding it difficult to rise and walk away.

John had invited her out on Saturday then he had quickly altered the invitation to Saturday week.

Obviously it was because he was already escorting Annette to some sort of function.

Helen's new-found happiness evaporated as she glanced over at the other

116

girl. No man was likely to prefer her company to Annette's. The older girl was so pretty . . .

She began to review her friendship with John Segreave, realising that she did not, as yet, really know him.

They had only just met, after all.

He was probably only being kind and helpful to a strange girl.

Indeed, her unusual search had probably attracted him much more than she had herself!

She thought about their date for Saturday week, feeling she ought to put it off. But no! She had promised to go, and would be happy to keep the date.

Though she mustn't read more into John Segreave's friendship than was there already.

She came out of her thoughts, startled, to realise that Moira had been talking and she hadn't heard a word.

'Oh! Sorry, Moira,' she said confusedly. 'I was daydreaming.'

'So you were!' Her friend laughed.

'We should have been back several minutes ago.'

'Goodness!' Helen hurriedly picked up her cardigan. 'Back to work then, Moira.'

Annette gave them a polite smile and a nod of recognition as they passed.

It didn't occur to Helen that the other girl had, perhaps, deliberately raised her voice a little as she talked . . .

On Saturday Helen had arranged to meet Moira in the afternoon and go to her home for supper.

'Mother's delighted to have you,' the other girl told her, with a smile, then made a rueful face. 'I've got a young brother and sister, too. I'm afraid you'll just have to put up with the noise they're sure to make.'

Helen grinned.

'I've got a young brother, too,' she told Moira, then her eyes quickly sobered.

Now and again she realised she was missing her own family quite a lot . . .

As she dressed to go out, she heard

voices downstairs. A moment later her landlady, Mrs Cathcart, came up to her bedroom.

* * *

'There's a young gentleman here to see you, Helen,' she announced. 'He says he's a friend of yours.'

The girl clipped on a pair of ear-rings to match her amber-coloured chunky beads and picked up her jacket and handbag before following Mrs Cathcart downstairs.

Alan McBride rose to greet her.

'I'm sorry to barge in on you, Helen,' he apologised with a quick smile. 'I had business in Prestwick today, and I remembered that your new address was nearby . . . ' He stopped, his smile fading a little. 'You're going out?'

'I'm afraid so,' she apologised. 'I've arranged to meet one of the girls who works with me, this afternoon. We're going shopping, then to her home for tea.'

Alan smiled again.

'I can see I've chosen the wrong day. Never mind. Perhaps I can walk with you to meet your friend.'

Mrs Cathcart beamed on both of them as they left. She liked to see her young guest going out and enjoying herself.

Moira was waiting when Helen turned up with Alan, and she introduced them.

'Alan and I are old friends. We lived near each other in Kilmarnock,' she explained.

'But now I find her too busy to speak to me,' he teased.

Moira looked up at him shyly.

'Please don't run away, Mr McBride.'

'Call me Alan,' he replied.

'Alan. I mean . . . We were only going to look at the shops, nothing very special.'

'Well, then, perhaps I can take you both out somewhere for a run before you go home. My car's parked nearby.'

Helen hesitated, but Moira was

looking delighted by the invitation.

'That would be lovely, wouldn't it, Helen? I mean, you would be able to see your friend after all.'

'Of course,' she agreed.

'Where will we go then?' asked Alan. 'Somewhere up the coast? Helen likes Troon. Would that do?'

'Not Troon,' Helen put in quickly, then coloured a little. 'I mean . . . we went there last time.'

'Could we go to Turnberry?' Moira was asking. 'My parents took us all there for a picnic a year or two ago, and it was such a happy day. I would love to go back.'

'Turnberry it is,' Alan agreed, and walked between the two girls to the car.

★   ★   ★

It was a happy afternoon, and Helen thought many times how nice Alan could be when he put himself out. He divided his attention naturally between herself and Moira.

Though there was a cool breeze from the sea, it was a pleasant afternoon and they found the walk near the sea front very bracing.

Moira admired the lovely gardens and the large hotel.

'You'll have to learn to play golf,' Alan teased, 'unless you play already.'

'No, I don't play. And I doubt if I'd be any good,' Moira returned. 'And I was pretty hopeless at tennis.'

'You must get Helen to coach you,' Alan advised. 'She's a lot better than I am, I'm afraid.'

'Rubbish,' protested Helen. 'You've always beaten me, Alan.'

He said nothing, but looked with a quick smile at Moira. For the first time that day, Helen felt a small stab of irritation.

Sometimes Alan had an oblique way of letting people know his accomplishments, and now he was trying it out on Moira.

'It's growing rather cold,' she said

briskly. 'Perhaps it's time we went back.'

'Of course.' Alan took an arm each as he led them back to the car.

'Please come home with us, Alan,' invited Moira as they reached Prestwick again.

'Oh, I mustn't gate-crash.'

'It isn't a party,' she protested, 'only supper with the family. Mother always cooks more than we need.'

'Well, if you're sure.'

'Yes, please do. You've been so kind, taking us out and . . . and I've enjoyed it.'

It had been a pleasant afternoon, Helen reflected, and she wasn't going to detract from Moira's enjoyment. Just the same, she would have to keep an eye on her friend to make sure she wasn't going to be hurt in any way.

She remembered her own attraction to Alan, and quite a number of heartaches before she got over it. It was easy to find him charming.

Mrs Bryden made the young couple

very welcome, and it was a happy evening, though rather late, by the time Alan offered to drive Helen home before going on to Kilmarnock.

They drove the short distance rather silently.

'Moira's an awfully nice girl,' Helen said at length.

'Yes, she seems nice,' Alan remarked absently, and again Helen felt quite irritated.

Alan's tone suggested that he had almost forgotten about the other girl already, whereas he had been going out of his way to be charming to her.

'Helen, I . . . ' he began.

'I wouldn't like Moira to be hurt . . . ever!' Helen spoke rather sharply.

She saw a glint in Alan's eyes.

'You wouldn't be jealous, would you, Helen?' he asked softly.

'No, I wouldn't,' she replied indignantly. 'I don't want her hurt, that's all.'

'She seems a nice sensible girl, well able to take care of herself,' said Alan. 'But I wouldn't mind you being jealous.

Are you still playing detective, Helen, or have you just decided to settle down in Prestwick?'

'I've still got some leads I want to pursue,' she told him rather coldly, feeling he was teasing her.

He took her hand and pressed it firmly.

'Then good luck, my dear. I'll come and see you again, though. Sometimes old friends are best, you know.'

She got out of the car and waved him away, thoughtfully.

Perhaps he was right about the old friends . . .

But he had been deliberately charming to Moira to try and make her jealous, or so she suspected. If that were so, he would only succeed in making her very angry.

*   *   *

Helen enjoyed the hustle and bustle of the busy airport, watching the joy of reunion among families, or the moments when tears were quietly shed after loved ones had parted.

She was kept busy at her own desk, and found the work more exhilarating than anything she had previously done.

As the days passed, she began to enjoy her independence from home.

Moira was proving to be a good companion.

Occasionally she would bring the conversation round, rather shyly, to Helen's earlier days in Kilmarnock, and her friendship with Alan McBride.

Helen was always rather non-committal about Alan . . .

The following Saturday evening John Segreave called for Helen in plenty of time for their date. He brought a pretty bunch of flowers for Mrs Cathcart, and a box of chocolates for herself.

Helen's landlady was very touched, and the girl could see the older woman's approval of her escort.

She, herself, felt grateful that John had been so thoughtful.

'I've been counting the days till this

evening,' he told her happily, and for a moment she glowed with pleasure.

Then she remembered Annette Thompson and withdrew a little.

'Have you?' she asked politely.

Some of the smile left John's eyes.

'Yes. I . . . I rather hoped you'd been looking forward to it as well.'

'Of course,' she agreed with a quick smile. 'It was nice of you to invite me.'

As they walked along the quiet streets, it was as though a constraint had fallen between them, and Helen did not enjoy the film as much as she'd expected she might.

She no longer felt at ease with John, aware that there might be heartache ahead if she allowed herself to enjoy his company too much.

Coming out of the cinema into the dark of the evening, John took her hand and tucked it firmly into his arm.

She stiffened involuntarily.

'What's the matter, Helen?' he asked, turning to look closely at her face.

'What do you mean?' she hedged.

'Don't slide back into your shell,' he told her. 'You know what I mean. You've always been carefree and happy, in spite of trying to work out your problem. What's wrong, Helen? It's as though you've put up a barrier between us. Why, Helen? Why?'

'I . . . I appreciate your taking me out,' Helen began hesitantly, 'but I know you've got other friends, too. You don't really have to make time for me, you know.'

She could sense that he was rather annoyed.

'Is that all our friendship means to you? The fact that we've got to make time for one another?'

'It's a very new friendship,' she said, in a low voice.

'But if you feel we're strangers, then surely the best way to get to know one another is to spend time in each other's company. Or don't you want to?'

She drew a deep breath.

'I thought you'd want to spend most of your free time with . . . with Annette

Thompson,' she managed. 'Surely she has more claims to your friendship than I.'

There was a heavy silence as they walked along side by side.

'So that's it!' John spoke quietly. 'If you really want to know . . . '

'I don't. It's none of my business.'

'I'd like to tell you anyway,' he insisted. 'The Thompsons and the Segreaves have been friends for many years, and I've known Annette since she was a schoolgirl.' He looked at her steadily.

'Didn't you once mention a young man you knew in Kilmarnock? An old friend?' he went on. 'But surely we can make new friends while we still see something of our old ones?'

* * *

Helen considered this, feeling rather foolish.

If she didn't want to become his friend, then how could she explain it was because she found him much too attractive for her own peace of mind.

'I suppose so,' she said, with a shy smile.

'Then cheer up, and let's enjoy ourselves. After all, it might not be long before you'll be rushing off back to Lancashire. Aunt Nan and Uncle William come home tomorrow night, then I'll be able to find out where Miss Armstrong lives.' He smiled.

'If she can't help you, then perhaps you ought to give up, and take your album back to the solicitor. He could employ someone to search for you. I don't think you should be wandering about on your own if the search takes you away from here. You're just a young girl, after all.'

'I'm old enough to take care of myself,' she said crisply, and a slow smile lit his eyes.

'You look about sixteen at the moment.'

Helen suddenly felt near to tears.

It was obvious now why John had

asked her out. He felt duty bound to keep an eye on her.

'We're home now,' she said, a trifle huskily. 'I'll say goodnight, Mr Segreave.'

'I thought you'd agreed to call me John.'

'John.'

He gripped her arm and she could see gentle amusement on his face.

'Don't be huffy, Helen. Now, give me a day or two to let Aunt Nan settle down. I know her, and she hates being quizzed about things. But I'll soon get Miss Armstrong's address out of her. It would be better if I ask her, because she might decide that anyone else was being nosey! I'd like you to meet her, though. Perhaps next Sunday afternoon?'

Helen had recovered her composure a little.

'That would be splendid,' she said quietly, 'though your aunt may not want to be bothered. I mean . . . if she doesn't like people asking her questions, she may not wish to see me.'

'I want her to get to know you,' John said firmly, 'as a friend of mine, not as someone delving into the past. She'd hate that.'

'Oh! I see.'

'Please just come on an ordinary visit to meet my Aunt Nan and Uncle William.'

'All right. Thank you, John.'

'And if I find out Miss Armstrong's address, I'll let you know.'

'Thank you. Goodnight.'

'Goodnight, Helen. I've enjoyed this evening. Have you?'

Helen nodded as she waved him away. But as she let herself into the house, her eyes sobered. She didn't know if she had enjoyed the evening . . .

Somehow her search had been taking second place recently. And this talk of Miss Armstrong had aroused her flagging interest.

But now she was remembering Gemmell Forbes again, his kindness to her, and the sad story of his early life.

She would do her best to fulfill his

wishes, she vowed.

In any case, it was something to occupy her mind, to keep herself from thinking too much about John Segreave.

A Casual Kiss

The following day Flora McGill came through from Auchinleck for a visit.

Both Helen and Mrs Cathcart were delighted to see her again, and had prepared a special tea in her honour.

'You're looking well, Helen,' Mrs McGill commented, looking critically at the girl.

She had acquired more poise, the older woman thought, though she wore a slightly reserved air, as if she'd suffered a disappointment of some kind.

'No more luck trying to find the lady you want to see?'

'A lead, but I sometimes feel it is a slender one. It was all such a long time ago, people tend to forget things,' Helen said ruefully. 'Anyway, I'll know in a week or two.'

'Will you go home then?'

'Well, I like being here,' Helen admitted, warm colour creeping into her cheeks, 'and I like my new job, though I'm not sure how long it will last. I'm happy to stay here for now.'

'And I'm happy to have her,' broke in Mrs Cathcart. 'How is everybody in Auchinleck?'

'Not so bad,' Flora answered, then eyed Helen again. 'There's a bit of sad news though, Helen. Old Mrs Mitchell has died. She passed away in her sleep the other morning. Her daughter got such a shock, poor woman, but Mrs Mitchell was getting on. I . . . I knew you would be sorry to hear about it, Helen.'

'I am,' the girl said sadly. 'I liked her. She had such spirit for her age.'

She had also been her strongest link with the past, Helen thought.

Now there was no-one who remembered the Turnbulls . . . unless it was Miss Armstrong!

'I must write to her daughter if you've got the address, Mrs McGill,' she decided. 'I'm very sorry she has gone.'

'Ay, it makes changes again. She was a good neighbour and a very fine woman. I'll leave the address with you.

'But what about your young man?' she asked, changing the subject.

Again Helen coloured.

'My . . . my young man?'

'Alan McBride. Have you seen much of him, or do you want me to mind my own business?'

'You were never good at that, Flora,' Mrs Cathcart said cheerfully, and the other woman merely smiled.

'He's still a friend,' Helen told her quietly.

Mrs McGill asked no more questions.

It was nice to see Helen looking well, but there was something bothering her, she decided shrewdly.

There was a spark of gaiety which was missing at the moment. But maybe the girl was just a little bit tired.

Helen found herself looking forward

to meeting John's aunt and uncle. She had seen him briefly during the week, and he told her that he'd obtained Miss Armstrong's address.

'Aunt Nan was rather curious, but I just told her I wanted to ask Miss Armstrong about something,' he explained. 'I don't like being deceptive, but she is inclined to be rather odd about some things. She hates poking and prying . . . ' He shrugged.

'I hope I'm not poking and prying,' Helen put in swiftly, the ready colour again in her cheeks. 'I only have to find Miss Agnes Turnbull. I don't want to know anything more about her, other than whether or not she had a sister, Edith, and knew Mr Gemmell Forbes.'

'We know that,' John told her. 'But try telling my Aunt Nan!'

Helen looked up at him shyly.

'I keep thinking how good you are to help me,' she said swiftly. 'I mean, it's not your responsibility.'

'I told you, I like doing it,' he assured

her, smiling warmly.

Helen returned his smile.

'I'm glad to accept your help,' she said quietly.

'Good. Well, Miss Armstrong doesn't live very far from Auchinleck. She has a cottage at Catrine. We could perhaps go there . . . say next Thursday evening? I'll ring her up and arrange it. It wouldn't take long to drive to Catrine, and I don't suppose it will take long for Miss Armstrong to decide if she can help us or not.'

Helen nodded, feeling excitement grip her once again.

For a time she had been dulled by disappointment when she found she had made a mistake over Mrs Segreave, but now she felt full of energy and enthusiasm.

How relieved she would be when she finally carried out the wishes of old Mr Forbes!

*   *   *

Nan Segreave was a small, rather plump lady with lovely curly white hair. With her round little face and tiny hands and feet, Helen thought she was one of the neatest ladies she had ever met.

Yet there was a lack of warmth to her, unlike William Segreave, John's uncle, who greeted Helen jovially.

'So you're a friend of John's,' he said approvingly. 'Well, you're very welcome, Miss . . . ?'

'Please call me Helen,' she glanced shyly at Mrs Segreave.

'You must come through to the fire,' the older woman was saying in her lilting accent. 'I think we're into winter now. I've felt the cold more since I got home from our business trip.'

'Yes, I knew you'd been away. Did you enjoy it?'

'I went mainly for my husband's sake,' Mrs Segreave said, with a sudden charming smile directed at her husband.

Helen looked on, thinking how nice

Mrs Segreave was when she softened up and smiled a little.

'I'm afraid I'm really a stay-at-home, though,' the older woman went on.

'Do you like it here, even though you belong to Moffat?' Helen asked.

'Oh, yes. I've lived in Prestwick since my marriage, though I've kept my Moffat accent . . . You're from Ayrshire surely, my dear?'

'Kilmarnock,' agreed Helen. 'Though my people . . . '

'Goodness it's cold,' interrupted John, as he breezed in after putting his car away. 'So you've all been getting acquainted? I'm very glad.'

'Do you work in the same department as John?' Mrs Segreave then asked the girl.

'No. I'm in the Freight Offices,' Helen told her with a smile. 'I love it, though.'

'So does John,' the older woman said with satisfaction.

Helen leaned back, feeling relaxed and at home. She felt regretful that Mrs

140

Segreave had not been the woman she wanted.

How nice it would have been to hand her the valuable stamp album, and to tell her that Mr Forbes had never forgotten her.

Tea was a delicious meal, and afterwards Helen helped with the washing up.

At first they tackled the job rather silently, then Helen managed to encourage Mrs Segreave to talk about the days when John first came to stay with them.

'He was always so clever,' his aunt said proudly. 'I knew he would make something of his life. He's just like my own son though I never had any children. I wasn't a young girl when I married, you see.'

'You must be happy to have John to stay with you then.'

'Yes. I only want his happiness,' Mrs Segreave said quietly. 'I shall only want for him what he wants for himself.'

It was rather late when John took Helen home, and he took her hand and swung it as they walked along.

'It's been a happy day,' she said with contentment. 'Thank you for asking me.'

'Thank you for coming,' he told her, his fingers tightening on her hand. 'Helen . . . I . . . '

He broke off, and she waited expectantly.

'What?'

'I was only going to say — I hope you like my aunt and uncle.'

'Oh, I do,' she assured him. 'It's nice to be with a family again. Sometimes I miss my home rather a lot, the noise, the bustle and fun and laughter.'

'I know,' John said softly. 'You must come home with me as often as you can. Goodnight, Helen.'

Swiftly he bent and kissed her, then he ushered her through the gate and strode off with a small wave.

Helen went indoors telling herself she must not pay too much attention to a casual kiss.

Yet it had been a happy day, and now

she could look forward to meeting Miss Armstrong on Thursday.

But suppose her search now took her away from Prestwick, what then? She would have to say goodbye to John Segreave, and that wouldn't be at all easy.

★ ★ ★

Two days later, Helen was hurrying to the canteen for a quick break when she passed John and Annette Thompson talking earnestly.

Annette's cheeks were flushed, and her eyes sparkled angrily, while John was looking embarrassed.

'But you said you'd come to the party, John,' she was saying. 'I asked you ages ago but now you say you've got to take this girl to Catrine. You can't just back out of things like that.'

'No, Annette, my dear, I . . . '

John's voice was lost amidst noise and bustle, and Helen hesitated, her cheeks glowing with colour.

How could John make arrangements to take her to see Miss Armstrong when he was already committed to Annette Thompson!

She felt embarrassed and paused, wanting to tell John he was quite free on Thursday evening and she could easily go to Catrine herself, but already Annette was walking away with her head in the air, and John was disappearing in the direction of the office.

The following evening John again called round to see her at Mrs Cathcart's.

'I've rung Miss Armstrong,' he told her with a smile, 'and she'll be pleased to see both of us on Thursday evening. Perhaps I could call for you at about seven-thirty?'

Helen felt her face go pale as she looked at him.

'There's no need for you to take me, John,' she said quietly. 'It's very good of you to arrange the interview with Miss Armstrong, but you needn't spend your time taking me. I know you'll have, well other things to do.'

She watched the smile leave his eyes.

'I told you before that I enjoy helping you with what you're doing. You must know that I admire you for making the effort.'

She saw that he was stumbling a little over the words, and suddenly found she wanted to explain about overhearing Annette's conversation with him.

But he had been annoyed last time she had mentioned Annette Thompson, and she had resolved since then to keep well out of his private affairs.

'Nevertheless, it is my task,' she insisted quietly. 'I think I can manage to handle it.'

This time his mouth tightened with anger.

'Very well. I'm sorry I intruded into something which is obviously your business. I was only trying to help.'

'Oh, no, it isn't that,' she said quickly.

'Then . . . ' He paused for a long moment. 'Then I can only assume my company isn't welcome. Perhaps ... perhaps you would prefer your friend in Kilmarnock to take you, Helen.'

He fumbled in his pocket for a scrap of paper.

'Here's the address of Miss Armstrong in Catrine. As I say, she'll be happy to see you on Thursday evening. I ... I've no doubt she'll have no objection to McBride going with you.

'I hope it's a fruitful visit, and that you manage to resolve your problem and find the lady you've been looking for very quickly.'

Helen was biting her lip to keep the tears away, wondering how she could correct the impression that she preferred Alan McBride's company to John's.

'Thank you,' she said huskily, taking the piece of paper. 'I ... I'll let you know how I get on.'

'That's all right, there's no need for you to bother.'

Helen watched him go, the tears brimming over.

Whatever had happened, she knew that she loved John Segreave and her heart ached over this rift between them.

But she couldn't accept his company for Thursday, when he had already promised to be somewhere else with Annette Thompson.

She just couldn't!

On Thursday evening Helen consulted the bus time table and decided that she could just manage the journey if she left work quickly, though she would have very little time with Miss Armstrong.

* * *

Miss Armstrong was tall and thin, and Helen could sense the reserve in her straight away, though she was welcomed cordially into the lovely cottage.

'I'm Helen Ferguson,' she explained when Miss Armstrong opened the door. 'John ... Mr Segreave ... phoned to ask if you'd see me.' She felt self-conscious now she was here.

'Yes, of course.' Miss Armstrong smiled briefly, then looked enquiringly up the garden path. 'Isn't John with you then, Miss Ferguson?'

'No, I thought I should like to come on my own.'

Some of the cordiality faded a little from Miss Armstrong's eyes.

'I see,' she said rather more coolly, and looked curiously at Helen. 'Please come into the sitting-room.'

It was a charming room, gay with chintz and soft pretty curtains, and faintly perfumed with flowers.

'What can I do for you, Miss Ferguson?' the older woman asked, as she offered Helen an easy chair near the fire, and went to pour tea from a trolley already set with small sandwiches and cakes.

'I . . . I'm trying to find a Miss Agnes Turnbull,' Helen said hurriedly. 'It's on behalf of an old gentleman called Gemmell Forbes . . .'

She stumbled on, doing her best to explain all about the valuable stamp album.

'He left a gift, the stamp album, which he wishes to go to Miss Turnbull. I promised to pass it on either to her, or any family she may have had.

'I heard from an old lady called Mrs Mitchell that you had known a Miss Turnbull, and she thought she was now Mrs Segreave.'

She paused for a moment, wishing that Miss Armstrong would show more interest, instead of sitting so coolly remote, drinking her tea.

'You see, the house where the Turnbulls lived became the property of your family after they left, and it was then turned into flats. Mrs Mitchell had one of the flats. She remembered you being bridesmaid to a Miss Agnes Turnbull who married a Mr Segreave, but it looks as if she got mixed up. The Miss Turnbull who is now Mrs Segreave, isn't the same lady who used to live in your old house.

'I see,' said Miss Armstrong, putting down her cup carefully. 'So you've been to Prestwick to ask her?'

'Yes.' Helen nodded. 'I was very disappointed. I would have liked the album to go to someone like Mrs Segreave, but now I've got to try to find another Miss Turnbull.

'That's why I've come to you, to ask you if you knew two ladies of the same name and if you knew the Miss Turnbull who used to live in Auchinleck.'

Miss Armstrong frowned thoughtfully, though she continued to look at Helen curiously.

'This is my last hope of finding Agnes Turnbull,' Helen told the woman. 'Can't you remember anything that might help?'

Miss Armstrong sighed a little.

'What a pity, because I really can't help you. This was all a very long time ago, and I've no memory for names or faces. I only kept in touch with Nan, who is now Mrs Segreave. I'm very sorry, Miss Ferguson.'

'I see.' Helen felt acutely disappointed. 'If you should happen to remember, would you please get in touch with me? I'll write down my address.'

'Certainly. But it was all a long time ago. I knew lots of girls then, but I never kept in touch.'

Well, this was the last of her possible leads and it had come to nothing, thought Helen. There was no point in looking further. She might as well go home and take the stamp album to the solicitor's office, as John had suggested.

Helen handed back her cup with thanks, and a sense of relief.

She rose to her feet, and buttoned up her coat.

'I'm so sorry to have been a nuisance,' she apologised.

'Not at all,' the older woman said, with a charming smile.

'Goodnight, Miss Armstrong.'

Helen made her way, disconsolately, to the bus stop.

What should she do now, she wondered. Give up and go home? Should she give in her notice at the airport?

Yet she was very happy in her job there, and she and Moira had become firm friends. She would miss her company.

But there was John . . . and Annette Thompson. If he had only been interested in her search, then wouldn't it be better for her to leave at once?

Helen was tired when she eventually reached Mrs Cathcart's, but she didn't sleep well that night.

Next morning she sent a small note to John Segreave, telling him that Miss Armstrong had been unable to help. Her memory of those days was far too clouded now, and she had only kept in touch with his aunt, she told him.

She posted the letter on her way to the airport.

★   ★   ★

The following weekend Helen was invited to go to Kilmarnock to stay with the McBrides, and she looked forward to this.

It hadn't been an easy week, and her own poor spirits seemed to have communicated themselves to Moira, who didn't seem to be her usual happy self.

Several times she seemed to be on the point of saying something to Helen, but she always turned away, and Helen felt she knew what the other girl had in mind.

Moira no doubt sensed that something was wrong, and wished to offer her help. However, Helen didn't feel like taking anyone into her confidence.

On Wednesday Moira seemed even quieter than usual, and Helen forgot about her own problems when she looked into her friend's white face.

'Are you feeling quite well, Moira?' she asked anxiously.

Moira nodded vigorously, then sat down on the nearest chair.

'No, I feel rather awful,' she confessed. 'It must be something I've eaten. I've an awful pain . . . '

'Shall I take you to see the nurse?'

'No, I'll be fine in a minute. Don't worry.'

But as the day wore on Moira began to feel really ill. She had to see a doctor, who quickly rang for an ambulance.

'It's your appendix, young lady,' he told her. 'Once that is removed, you'll be right as rain in no time.'

'Oh, dear.' Moira groaned. 'Oh, Helen . . . '

'Don't worry. I can take on extra work till you're better again, and I'll let your parents know. Your mother and father will be able to see you in hospital.'

'Thank you,' she whispered uneasily, and Helen hoped the ambulance would hurry.

'Helen, I . . . '

'It's all right, dear. I'll see to everything.'

'But . . . it's not all right,' her friend

cried. 'I . . . I was going out with Alan McBride on Thursday. I've been trying to tell you, Helen.'

Tears were starting in Moira's eyes, and Helen pressed her hand to reassure her.

'Well, I can let Alan know, too. That can soon be resolved. Don't worry about that.'

'But . . . you don't mind?'

Helen bit her lip. She didn't mind for her own sake, but she minded very much if Alan was seeing Moira in any sort of casual way.

'No, of course not,' she said cheerfully. 'Here's the ambulance now. Don't worry about a thing. I'll see Alan for you.'

'Thanks, Helen,' whispered Moira, gratefully.

Helen quickly informed Moira's parents and that evening, when she rang the hospital, she found that Moira's appendix had been removed and she was now 'comfortable.'

Helen sighed with relief, and lifted

the phone again to ring Alan McBride in Kilmarnock.

However, after allowing the number to ring for a few minutes, she put down the receiver reluctantly. Obviously there was no-one in. She turned away thoughtfully. Alan was meeting Moira at the airport the following evening, and it rather looked as though she would have to be there, in Moira's place.

She didn't really like the idea that she would be meeting Alan in those circumstances, but it couldn't be helped.

He would have to be told what had happened to Moira.

In any case, thought Helen, as she walked home to Mrs Cathcart's, it might be as well for her to see Alan, and try to guess if his friendship with Moira was becoming important to him.

She hoped very much that it was, because it seemed to her that it had become very important to Moira.

Quiet And Moody

The following evening Helen was waiting patiently for Alan at the appointed time, when she saw John pass by in his car. She watched the car slow to a stop, as John found a convenient place to park, then the car door opened and he climbed out, glancing in her direction.

Helen's heart beat more quickly, and she watched him nervously.

She had not seen him since he had given her Miss Armstrong's address, and many times she wondered if she had done the right thing.

Had he kept his date with Annette after she had left the evening free for him?

She suspected that he had, since Annette seemed so gay and carefree these days.

But now he was coming towards her

purposefully, stopping to allow cars to pass.

A moment later, however, Helen felt a hand touching her arm, and looked round to see Alan standing beside her.

'Hello, Helen,' he said quietly. 'Waiting for someone?'

'Oh, Alan!' she cried with relief. 'I'm — glad to see you. I'm waiting for you, as a matter of fact.'

'Now I'm really flattered!'

'But . . . '

Helen turned again, quickly, to look for John, and her heart sank when she saw him turn round and stride towards his car again.

He climbed in and shut the door with a bang.

'Have I frightened off your new boyfriend?' Alan asked teasingly.

'He's not my new boyfriend,' Helen replied rather sharply, though there was a bleak look in her eyes.

She turned again to her companion.

'I'm afraid you're going to be disappointed though, Alan. Moira can't meet you tonight. She's in hospital . . . '

'In hospital!' Alan's face whitened with alarm, and relief caught at Helen's heart.

So Alan did care for Moira!

'Don't worry,' she said gently. 'It's appendicitis. She's had her operation and is going to be all right.'

'Oh, that's good.'

For a moment he looked rather sheepish, then he grinned down at her.

'I'm so glad. I've . . . er . . . been seeing Moira now and again, Helen, since you weren't too eager for my company.'

'Yes, I know.'

'She's rather nice.'

Helen grinned impishly.

'Yes, I know,' she repeated. 'I'm so glad, Alan. Now, if we hurry, we'll still be in time for visiting. I'm sure Moira's parents won't mind if we see her for a few minutes.'

'Can we get fruit and flowers?' asked Alan anxiously. 'I've only brought her chocolates.'

'I'm sure she'll be delighted with those,' Helen told him.

At the hospital Helen was pleased to see Moira looking better. She only stayed for a few moments, to allow Alan and Moira to have a little time alone.

As she sat waiting in the car for Alan, Helen relived the moment when she saw John turn back to his car after he saw Alan.

She thought about Annette, and wondered if she might have made a dreadful mistake in keeping out of John's private affairs.

Suppose he really only felt friendship and affection for Annette, as he had hinted once before!

★ ★ ★

Helen was kept very busy at her job, helping out with the work which Moira usually did.

It was a challenge to her, and she enjoyed that.

She had gone up to Kilmarnock at

the weekend, finding Alan cheerfully contented, though Mrs McBride was rather quiet and subdued, as if she had a lot on her mind.

However, Helen soon had her smiling happily again, when she began to tell her about her new job, mentioning Moira quite a few times, and always in a complimentary way.

'Alan wants to bring Moira Bryden home to meet me,' the older woman told Helen, as they washed up together.

'I know. I'm so glad.' Helen smiled warmly. 'She's a lovely girl and my best friend. Alan is very lucky.'

Mrs McBride looked at her earnestly.

'I don't quite know how to say this, but at one time I had hoped . . . '

'I know. But we're just good friends, Mrs McBride. We always will be, I suppose, but never anything more.'

The older woman sighed.

'Then I'm thankful he's found a nice girl. He was so restless for a while. I think that was because of you.'

Helen coloured.

'I'm sorry.'

'Oh, well, we can't organise people's lives for them. I'll welcome Moira when she comes.' Mrs McBride's manner was more relaxed.

Helen nodded, her eyes rather wistful.

There was only happiness ahead for Moira and Alan. But her own future wasn't so bright.

* * *

On Saturday Helen went out shopping for Mrs Cathcart. It had been a rather long week; a trifle lonely with Moira away and no hope of seeing John.

Helen took a good look at her life, and decided that to go home was the best plan.

As soon as Moira returned to work, and she could leave without inconvenience, she would do just that.

Her 'temporary' job had already lasted quite a while . . .

In the meantime she stayed on with

Mrs Cathcart, finding the older woman cheerful and motherly.

'I'll do the shopping, since you are busy baking,' Helen had offered.

'That would be a help, dear,' Mrs Cathcart told her gratefully. 'I don't need much, but I'm nearly out of salt, and I can't do without that.'

It was while Helen was having a quick cup of coffee in a small tearoom, her purchases completed, that there was a touch on her arm.

She turned to look at a small plump lady sitting at the next table.

'Mrs Segreave!' she exclaimed. 'Why, how nice!'

'Hello, my dear. We haven't seen you for some time. I asked John but he said you were busy doing someone else's work.'

'That's right,' Helen replied. 'My friend, Moira Bryden, is in hospital, but she's doing very well. I . . . '

She broke off, wondering what to say.

'I'm sorry I haven't called on you,' she finished.

'Wouldn't you like to join me?' invited Mrs Segreave.

Helen rose quickly and transferred her cup of coffee to the next table.

'I never interfere in John's affairs, and I expect him to keep out of mine,' the older woman said quietly, though her smile made the words seem warmer. 'Only, I hope you haven't quarrelled. He's been moody recently, though he does his best not to allow his moods to affect the family.'

'I see,' said Helen, soft colour rising in her cheeks. 'No, we haven't quarrelled. We ... we're not really close friends, you know. I have no demands on his time.'

'Oh!'

'Surely he and Annette are ... well ... special friends?'

Mrs Segreave eyed her shrewdly.

'They've known each other since they were children, but John has never hinted that there is anything more. Wouldn't you like to come round for tea one evening?'

Helen bit her lip. It was very kind of Mrs Segreave to invite her. But what would John think if she accepted the invitation?

'It's very kind of you,' she said slowly, 'but . . . '

'Ah, here's John now!' Mrs Segreave smiled at him as he approached. 'I've just been talking to Helen. We've had a cup of coffee, and I've invited her to come to tea next week. That would be nice, wouldn't it?'

'Very nice.' John spoke stiffly, and Helen's eyes clouded as she turned away.

'I'm afraid . . . '

'You've got a date with Alan McBride,' John finished flatly.

'Alan McBride has just become engaged to Moira,' Helen explained quietly. 'And I'm very happy for them both. Well, I must go home with this shopping for Mrs Cathcart.'

She bent to pick up her shopping bag.

'I'm sorry but I'll be busy during the

week visiting Moira, Mrs Segreave, though it's very nice of you to ask me.'

'No. You can't be busy every evening,' John interrupted urgently. 'Can't you keep one evening free?'

Helen felt a sudden surge of happiness at the warmth of his tone, and the pressure of his fingers on her own.

'All right,' she agreed, 'which night would suit?'

'Tuesday?' Mrs Segreave suggested.

'I'll come for you, Helen,' John offered. 'There are a few things I want to talk over, anyway.'

'All right,' she agreed again.

Helen walked away from the café, feeling that her world had suddenly righted itself.

She no longer wanted to go back home, even though she was beginning to forget about her original purpose in coming to Prestwick.

But John Segreave didn't wait for Tuesday before seeing Helen again. That following afternoon he called at Mrs Cathcart's and invited Helen to go out for a walk. She changed into warm outdoor clothing, and they set off together into the crisp, fresh air, faintly perfumed with the tang of the sea.

After a while John found a quiet place where they could sit and talk.

★   ★   ★

'You don't really mind that your friend and Alan McBride are engaged?'

'Oh, that! I'd only just heard about it yesterday,' Helen told him. 'Moira's out of hospital now, and Alan celebrated by buying her a ring. I think both families are delighted.'

'But you don't mind?'

'No, of course not. I've known Alan all my life. At one time I was attracted to him, but that meant nothing. I think there is always a bond between childhood friends, people we've known all our lives.'

'Yes.'

John's tone was very thoughtful.

'Yet you didn't seem to want to

become friends with me,' he said after a while.

She coloured. It was a few moments before she replied.

'I thought you were just being kind to me, and that it might be making things difficult between you and Annette.

'I overheard her reminding you about an appointment with her on the night you had arranged to take me to see Miss Armstrong.'

John frowned, his eyes puzzled.

'You overheard . . . ' He broke off for a moment. 'Yes, it was a sherry party her parents were giving in aid of the Red Cross. But didn't you hear me tell Annette she was mistaken? I didn't agree to go to that party. I bought a ticket, but only as a form of donation.'

'I see.' Helen felt suddenly guilty. 'I . . . I'm sorry, John.'

He took her hand.

'We've been at cross purposes, my dear. Annette means about the same to me as Alan McBride does to you. But I'm not going to marry her, and I don't suppose she would want me even if I did propose.'

Helen said nothing. She wasn't so sure about that!

'Why don't we see something of each other?' John urged. 'Don't you think we could become good friends . . . even something more in time?'

'Perhaps,' said Helen softly.

John bent to kiss her firmly, then pulled up her coat collar as they began to walk back towards Mrs Cathcart's.

'See you on Tuesday,' he said as they parted.

'All right, John,' she agreed.

★   ★   ★

The next week or two were the happiest Helen had known. Mrs Segreave made her very welcome, laughingly declaring that John was now much easier to live with.

'Oh, dear,' he said contritely. 'Was I moody, Aunt Nan?'

'You weren't yourself,' she replied. 'I

don't like to see things go wrong for you.'

He grinned sheepishly, but Helen could see the affection he felt for his aunt.

'You spoil me,' he told her, pulling one of her white curls.

'You must ask your parents to come down to Prestwick to visit us some Sunday, my dear,' Mrs Segreave said to Helen later, as they washed up together.

'Well, it's rather a long way at the moment,' Helen answered.

'From Kilmarnock? Surely not.'

'Oh, they moved recently. They're living in Bolton now, in Lancashire.'

There was heavy silence for a moment, and Helen heard the other woman catch her breath.

'Bolton!' she repeated. 'Then, you're from Bolton? Did you come North again because of your job?'

'No, I came to find a Miss Agnes Turnbull. That's how I got to know John, because I found out that was your maiden name.

'Only you aren't the lady I want to find. My Miss Turnbull had a sister called Edith. I promised an old friend of mine, Mr Gemmell Forbes, that I'd try to find her.

'He's dead now, I'm afraid, but I'm still trying to carry out his wishes. Only, I've no more leads now.'

'So you're the girl who's been asking all those questions!' Mrs Segreave had her back to Helen but now she turned to face her angrily.

'My last hope was Miss Armstrong from Catrine, but she couldn't do anything for me at all.'

'You went to see Miss Armstrong?' cried Mrs Segreave.

Helen saw with surprise that the older woman was really angry.

'Why, yes,' she stammered. 'John got me her address from you, Mrs Segreave. I rather thought you knew all this.'

'He told me a girl from England was looking for someone with the same name as myself. But I strongly object to

171

my friends being questioned in this way. I don't like people poking and prying into private affairs.'

'Oh, but I wasn't ... I had no thought of any such thing. It's in Miss Turnbull's interest after all.'

Helen's mouth had gone dry. She remembered a long time ago that John had warned her that his Aunt Nan had some sort of aversion to being asked about her personal affairs.

Now she seemed to have put her foot in it with her!

For the rest of the evening Mrs Segreave seemed very quiet and moody, and bade Helen a rather cool good-night.

John's eyes were puzzled a little as he looked from one to the other.

* * *

'You and Aunt Nan ... you didn't quarrel, did you?' he asked Helen later.

'No,' she assured him. 'Not really. But she got annoyed when she found out I'd been to see Miss Armstrong.'

'Oh, dear, that's her pet hate,' he told her ruefully. 'I should have warned you not to say anything. She's got a thing about it.'

'Well, I am sorry,' said Helen, 'but I only told her exactly what had happened.'

'She'll come round,' John assured her. 'She never stays out of temper for long.'

But although Mrs Segreave was quite polite to Helen on the next occasion they met, she was a lot more reserved than she had been previously.

Soon John began to realise there was a lack of warmth between Helen and his aunt. But the older woman refused to acknowledge that her attitude towards Helen had changed in any way.

'I welcome her as I welcome all your friends, John,' she said, looking rather hurt. 'If Helen has been complaining . . .'

'She hasn't.' John broke in quickly.

'Well, perhaps you're imagining things. She seems a nice enough young lady, but lots of girls are these days. I think they're better educated and better dressed than we were ... '

John excused himself, unwilling to sit and listen to Aunt Nan talking about general things.

He said nothing to Helen, but she sensed his uneasiness.

Helen pushed all her worries to the back of her mind for Moira's engagement party. Her friend asked her to bring John along and they spent a very happy evening.

On the way home, however, John was more silent than usual, though he bade Helen goodnight as warmly as ever.

She watched him go thoughtfully.

As she prepared for bed, she resolved to have things out with Mrs Segreave as soon as she could.

Perhaps the older woman didn't realise that she was clouding their happiness by this strange attitude.

The girl chose an evening when she

knew John was working late, and called round to see his aunt.

She was relieved to find her on her own.

* * *

'John is at work,' Mrs Segreave explained to Helen. 'I'm afraid you've called at the wrong time.'

'I don't want to speak to John, Mrs Segreave, I would rather like a word with you.'

'Oh?' The older woman seemed surprised.

'I would like to . . . to clear the air between us.'

'I don't understand.' Mrs Seagreave frowned.

'I feel that you've changed towards me . . . ' Helen began.

'Surely you're imagining things!'

'No. I feel the change in your attitude towards me. So does John, and it's making him rather unhappy.'

Mrs Segreave nodded.

'I do regret going to see Miss Armstrong and involving a friend of yours in my affairs,' Helen went on. 'But it could be that Miss Armstrong knows my Miss Turnbull, too. Let me tell you about it . . . please . . . '

'There's no need.'

'I think there is. Only by knowing everything will you be able to understand my motives. I'm doing my very best to carry out the last wishes of a gentleman who was very dear to me.'

Quickly she told Mrs Segreave about Mr Forbes, and the tragic loss of his young wife. She explained about the valuable stamp album and her last real lead, which had come from old Mrs Mitchell.

'She remembered that Miss Armstrong, who came to live in the Turnbulls' house, knew Miss Agnes Turnbull. Only there she became confused and thought she had become a Mrs Segreave.

'We think Miss Armstrong knew two Miss Turnbulls, only she says she had a bad memory for names. She's only kept in touch with you, she told me when I called. I . . . I suppose you didn't know another girl with the same name as yourself, who lived in that house?

'You see, I don't want the album, either. I feel it belongs to old Mr Forbes' sister-in-law and any family she may have.'

Mrs Segreave had listened quietly to her explanation.

'I . . . ' She began to reply.

The door flew open suddenly and William Segreave breezed in.

'It's a cold night,' he informed them. 'Hello, Helen. Are you staying to supper?'

'Yes, please do,' said his wife.

Her hostile attitude seemed to have softened a little, but there was still no smile in her eyes.

Helen suddenly remembered that Mrs Segreave was not an Ayrshire woman, and wouldn't know which house she meant in Auchinleck. There would be no point in asking her any more questions.

'No. I can't stay,' she said rising. 'I only came to talk a little.'

'Very well. I won't keep you,' said Mrs Segreave. 'Wrap up well before you leave.'

'Shall I walk home with you?' her husband offered.

'Oh, no, I'll be all right alone. Goodnight.'

Helen walked home thoughtfully. Had she cleared the air, or only made things worse?

She had no idea. She would have to wait and see . . .

Another thought struck her as she entered the house. If Mrs Segreave had got married in Moffat, how did old Mrs Mitchell know about the wedding?

Helen slowly mounted the stairs to her bedroom. No doubt the old woman had remembered Miss Armstrong being bridesmaid at the wedding.

Dare she visit Miss Armstrong again, she wondered, then shrank a little from the idea. She was certainly not a lady who liked to be questioned.

John had seen Helen leaving the house. Though he called to her, she didn't hear and hurried off down the avenue.

He tackled her about it the following evening.

'I went to have a word with your aunt,' she explained. 'I felt that there was something wrong between us . . . that perhaps I had offended her in some way. I wondered if she would tell me what it was, if I got her on her own.'

'She says it's just imagination.' John smiled.

'I know. Maybe now that she has got to know me better, she just doesn't like me.'

Helen bit her lip, turning away from him.

'Oh, this time I am sure it is your imagination,' he told her, taking her hand. 'I'm sure she's fond of you, Helen.'

'Do you really think so?'

'Sure of it.' He sounded quite

positive. 'It wouldn't make any difference between us, would it?'

Helen shook her head slowly, but her eyes were troubled when they met his. Close family ties meant as much to her as they did to John.

* * *

The next few days seemed long to Helen, and she felt that some of the joy had gone out of her life.

She and John had been so happy in one another's company, but now they were both quieter and more thoughtful.

Then one morning Helen received a short note from Mrs Segreave asking her to call and see her the following evening.

I would like to talk to you privately, she wrote, *and I would be most grateful if you could come and see me. I look forward to our talk, as there has been much on my mind of late. If you can't come, perhaps you could telephone and let me know.*

Helen read the note through twice then put it carefully in her handbag. She would be happy to visit Mrs Segreave, she decided, and perhaps she would learn just why things had changed between them.

Her welcome the following evening was much more like old times.

John's aunt seemed genuinely glad to see her, and ushered her into the comfortable sitting-room.

'John is out this evening at his Photography Club, but I expect you know that.'

'Yes, it's the one interest we can't share,' Helen agreed. 'I can't aim straight with a camera at all.'

'Nor can I,' said Mrs Segreave. 'I cut off William's head in the photographs I took on that business trip! Now, my dear, let's have tea, then I'll tell you what is on my mind.'

'What About The Baby?'

'It's difficult for me to begin,' Mrs Segreave said at length, 'and I suppose the best way is by confessing that I rather misled you. When John asked if I knew Gemmell Forbes, I said I didn't. In a way that was true. I never met him. But . . . but he did know my sister.'

Helen started, looking at the older woman in surprise.

'Then . . . '

'Yes,' Mrs Segreave said quietly. 'I'm the Agnes Turnbull you've been looking for. I suppose if you'd thought about it clearly, you would have seen it was so all along.'

'I was awfully puzzled . . . '

'Yes. I thought you must be, and I'm very sorry. I denied it because I didn't want to remember a past which . . . which was rather tragic for me.'

Mrs Segreave put down her teacup a

trifle unsteadily.

'I loved my sister Edith. She was a very beautiful girl and we had always been close. When she was eighteen she met a young man and fell in love. She kept their meeting quiet, even from me.

'But I found out one night when she was going to meet him and it was then she swore me to secrecy. She said our parents would not approve of him and would force her to give him up.

'Well, I kept quiet, and for a while I knew she was wildly happy. I thought it was too bright a flame to last long, and that it would burn itself out.

'Later when she suddenly went quiet and listless, I thought he had left her. I know now that Mr Forbes must have gone to England at that time.'

'I think he found it just as difficult to leave her,' Helen put in softly.

'Yes, I can see that. But all we knew was that Edith's high spirits had drooped. She became quiet and rather pale. Mother was very worried about her. She thought Edith was needing a tonic, and wanted to take her to the doctor. But she would have none of it.

'Then one afternoon she was hurrying home with some shopping and . . . and rushed across the road to the house. She didn't see the car which hit her.'

Mrs Segreave's voice trembled.

'She was taken to hospital, and it was then we found out she was having a child. Father and Mother were distracted, and tried to get the best doctors possible for Edith. She was transferred to a hospital in Dumfries where several operations were performed.

'They prolonged her life till her daughter was born a few months later. But Edith died a few hours after the birth.'

'Mrs Segreave . . . '

'Please, let me finish. Then, perhaps, you'll understand. We didn't know Edith was married. Young Mr Forbes came to see Father a week or two after Edith was knocked down.

'It was then that Father knew who . . . who Edith had been meeting. He was so angry and heartbroken, he didn't tell him about the baby, and allowed him to think Edith was lost to him for always. Father was a hard man . . . a very hard man.'

'Oh, Mrs Segreave,' whispered Helen, 'if only Mr Forbes had known.'

'I know.' There was pain in the older woman's voice. 'I can only tell you what it was like from our point of view. It must be difficult for you to understand all this, but it might have been easier if you had known Father.

'As I say, he was a strong man . . . and very hard. He would have been black with fury if he had known about the marriage before . . . before it all happened.'

★ ★ ★

Helen asked the one question she had been longing to ask.

'And the baby? What about the baby,

Mrs Segreave? Did she live?'

The older woman nodded.

'That's what has made it so difficult for me over the past few days. Father found a nice couple to foster the baby. They lived in a pretty village near Moffat.

'We had moved near there from Auchinleck, you see, after Edith's accident, and he bade me forget about our life in Ayrshire, as though it had never existed.

'Father and Mother used to go and see the baby, but I wasn't allowed to have anything to do with it. I tried hard to find out where Edith's baby was, and who was looking after her, but I couldn't.

'I thought they must have chosen a foster home miles away. Later I found out it was fairly near.

'It was only after Father died, two years after Mother, that I found an address. But when I went there, they had moved away.'

There was silence for a while.

'I shall have to look through all my papers to find that address again. It was a long time ago, and they had already left that house when I tried,' she went on thoughtfully.

'I'd always thought Father was comfortably off, but there wasn't a great deal of money when he died. I had to sell up our house in Moffat, but with the money I had, I was still quite comfortable.

'Afterwards I met my husband and married. I told William all about Edith, and the baby. We thought about trying to find her again with a view to adoption, though she would be growing into a youngster by then. I also thought about the foster mother who no doubt loved the child, and I knew I couldn't take her away.

'Later I had John to love and as the years passed I managed to put Edith's daughter to the back of my mind.'

There was silence for a few moments, then Mrs Segreave leaned forward.

'Are you willing to go to Moffat and

try to trace her, Helen? If by some miracle, you do find her, could you . . . ?' Mrs Segreave choked, and tears flooded her eyes.

Helen put a comforting hand on her arm.

'Of course. I'm sure she'll want to see you, and be delighted to know she has a family of her own.'

'All those wasted years,' Mrs Segreave murmured sadly.

'I know.'

Helen sat back in her chair, her mind spinning. Now that her search was on again, and this time for Mr Forbes' daughter, she felt her old eagerness returning.

But what about her job? And John? Perhaps she would have to say goodbye to both of them for some little time.

* * *

John Segreave was very annoyed when later that evening he found out that his aunt was Miss Turnbull after all. He'd arrived home to find Helen still there. His aunt quickly explained.

'But you said you'd never known anyone called Gemmell Forbes,' he put in reproachfully.

'That was true, or half true at any rate,' his aunt replied. 'I've explained to Helen why I didn't want to be reminded of the past, John. My first reaction was to deny all knowledge of Mr Forbes.'

'It's made things much more difficult for Helen,' John protested.

'I know, dear, but you see . . . I was ashamed of the way Father behaved over Edith's baby. I can't expect you to understand, but . . . ' Her voice trailed off lamely.

John was silent for a moment.

'Perhaps I do understand,' he said at length.

He turned to Helen.

'What happens now?'

'When Mrs Segreave finds that address in Moffat, I'll go there, and try to find out where Mr Forbes' daughter went after there. What is her name, by the way?' Helen turned to the older woman questioningly.

'She was called Rose and the people who adopted her were called Fielding, so her name will be Rose Fielding. Of course, she may be married by now. No doubt she is, because she'll be in her forties.'

They were silent for a while, thinking about the woman who would now have to be found.

'What about your job at the airport?' John asked abruptly, turning to Helen.

She bit her lip.

'I know. I think I'll have to give it up, if the search is going to take some time. It was only supposed to be temporary anyway. I'll have to stay in Moffat, you see.'

'Won't you need another job?'

'Yes,' she said reluctantly. 'I couldn't stay long without trying to find a job.'

'Well, don't give up your job till you find out if the search will take a long time,' John advised. 'I mean, you could find the lady you're looking for quite quickly. Couldn't we take a trip down to Moffat, just to see what we can find out?'

'We?' asked Helen, smiling.

'I'd prefer to come with you, to see you safely settled. I mean, it's all strange to you at the moment.'

'It was strange to me when I came here first,' she pointed out, and John flushed a little.

'I'm sorry,' he said stiffly. 'I ought not to interfere.'

'No. It isn't that,' she put in quickly, 'and I am grateful for your concern. But I can manage quite well myself. You tend to treat me like a child sometimes, John.'

Mrs Segreave looked from one to the other. They were all tired, as it had been an upsetting evening emotionally.

She could see that while John didn't want to lose sight of Helen, the girl liked to be recognised as capable and independent.

'Suppose you drive Helen down to

Moffat next Sunday,' she suggested to John, 'then you can make plans after seeing how the land lies. I would like you to find my niece, and perhaps explain things to her a little, before I meet her. I'm only ashamed that I haven't tried harder to find her again all these years.'

'What about it, Helen?' John queried.

'All right,' she agreed.

★　★　★

It was a rather cold, crisp morning when Helen and John left Prestwick and set off on the road to Moffat.

'We'll have to make it early,' John decided. 'It isn't a straight-forward journey from here, but I think we ought to go through Muirkirk and Douglas, then on to the A74. I asked Aunt Nan, but it's some time since she made the journey, so she wasn't much help.'

Helen checked in her handbag to make sure she had the piece of paper with the Fieldings' old address on it.

'Foxholes Cottage,' she read. 'It sounds a nice address. Mrs Segreave says it's a few miles on the other side of Moffat, towards Wamphray. She thinks the Fieldings will be in their seventies by now. Maybe they moved away from Moffat altogether, John.'

'That's what we have to find out,' he said, glad that the main roads were quiet in the early morning. 'But we may be lucky.'

'I hope we can find Miss Fielding, for your aunt's sake as much as anybody's,' Helen went on. 'I think it's something which has worried her for years.'

'I know,' John replied. 'Maybe because it was such an upsetting time for her that she wants to forget all about it.

'Look, Helen, what's going to happen if you find Miss Fielding straight away? I don't mean the fact that we can put her and Aunt Nan in touch with one another. I mean it's time we thought of our future, Helen.'

Helen sat still beside him, wondering

if John was going to mention marriage.

Her heart beat a little bit faster as she glanced sideways at him, knowing that she cared enough to accept him.

She didn't really want to go home and leave him now.

'I . . . I don't know,' she said huskily. 'But . . . '

'But what?'

Helen searched for words. Surely it was up to John to suggest plans for them both. She couldn't find the words to tell him how much it would hurt her to leave him.

Then she saw that John was concentrating on driving the car through traffic, and the precious moment seemed to be lost.

'But you think we should concentrate on one thing at a time,' finished John, and she made no reply.

Perhaps he was right. Their personal affairs could wait till she had found Miss Fielding.

Yet . . . could he really care very much for her when he was content to leave things like that?

Helen withdrew a little into her shell, and there was little conversation between them till they reached Moffat.

John found a quiet place where they could eat the lunch Mrs Segreave had packed for them.

'This coffee is good,' said Helen. But now that she was so near the end of her search, she felt nervously excited and was unable to do full justice to the meal.

'Have another sandwich,' John offered.

She shook her head.

'No thanks. I'm too excited. Somehow it's even more exciting looking for Mr Forbes' daughter than his sister-in-law. It will be lovely if I can hand over that stamp album to her.'

'I'd like to look at it before you do hand it over,' John mentioned.

'All right,' she agreed, 'though I'm afraid I can't really appreciate it. What about you?'

'I know nothing about stamps. But it intrigues me that we're going to all this trouble over something we've merely talked about. It would be interesting to see it, that's all.'

'If it hadn't been for Miss Fielding, it might be yours one day,' said Helen, thoughtfully. 'Your Aunt Nan would probably pass it on to you.'

'Well, I don't want it,' John told her flatly. 'I wouldn't feel that it belonged to me, somehow, any more than you feel it belongs to you.' He looked at her with a smile.

'Let's hope that we do find Rose Fielding and settle the matter. I think she's the best person to claim ownership.'

'I agree.' Helen was packing away the food they hadn't wanted. 'Should we ask the way from now on?'

'Perhaps that would be best,' John agreed.

★ ★ ★

It took them quite a while to find Foxholes Cottage.

Almost an hour later, John drew up the car outside a solid redbrick house with a neat garden. It wasn't quite the pretty cottage Helen had imagined.

'It looks very sturdy anyway,' she said to John. 'It's probably a very comfortable house.'

'Come on. Let's talk to whoever lives here now. Keep your fingers crossed that it's someone old enough to have taken over from the Fieldings.'

He rang the bell, and from inside the house Helen could hear the happy shouts of children at play. Her heart beat faster. At least there appeared to be someone at home.

The door flew open and a youngish woman stood there, a rather splashed apron tied round her waist, and her hair escaping from hairpins.

'Yes?' she asked.

'We are trying to trace people who once lived here called Fielding,' said

Helen. 'I wonder if the name means anything to you?'

The young woman looked mystified for a moment, then shook her head.

'No, I'm sorry, I've never heard of them. My name is Jameson.'

Helen was getting used to being given a disappointing answer, and no longer gave up so easily.

'Er . . . have you lived here all your life, Mrs Jameson?' she asked. 'I mean, could it have been your parents' home before yours? These people lived here a good many years ago.'

'How many years?' asked Mrs Jameson, then glanced over her shoulder as a baby started to cry.

'You'd better come in,' she said hurriedly.

Helen and John thanked her as they followed her into a cosy, but untidy, living-room, where three small children were playing.

A baby lay kicking in a pram, having struggled half out of his harness.

Young Mrs Jameson fumbled with

the straps to undo them, before picking up the baby.

'How many years did you say?' she asked.

'About forty.'

The girl's eyebrows rose.

'Goodness! That's a long time. No, we've been here for eight years now, ever since Colin and I got married. Before that . . . '

She wrinkled her brows.

'No, it's no use. The name will come to me, because we kept getting post for the previous people after we moved in. Clark? That's it! Mr and Mrs Clark.'

'Did you live around here before you married?' asked Helen, and young Mrs Jameson shook her head.

'No, I belong to Thornhill. But my husband was born in Moffat. He's out at the moment.'

Helen glanced at John.

'Will he be long?' he asked.

'He should be home around three o'clock,' Mrs Jameson told him.

'Then may we come back and talk to him?' John asked. 'We've come rather a long way to find Miss Fielding,' he added.

'Of course, I'm sure he'll be glad to talk to you,' the young woman told him.

Helen found herself being regarded gravely by two small girls, each of them hugging a doll.

'Hello,' she said grinning. 'Are you playing 'House'?'

The elder giggled shyly, and nodded.

'Here's something to put on your dolly's teaset,' she said, producing a box of sweets.

The children fell on the sweets with glee, and Helen felt John's gaze on her and blushed a little.

'I've played 'House' often in the past,' she said to Mrs Jameson with a smile. 'It was always nice to have 'cakes' for tea.'

'May I offer you a cup?' the young woman asked, looking slightly harassed, but trying to be hospitable.

'Oh, no, thank you. We'll come back,' said Helen hurriedly.

'I'll tell Colin then, when he comes home,' Mrs Jameson said as she showed them out.

Did He Really Care?

'Somehow I didn't think it would be easy,' said Helen with a sigh, as they climbed back into the car. 'I remember what it was like before. I always had to question somebody else!

'I suppose that's why I feel I have to do it on my own, and not get you involved, John. It can be awfully frustrating, you know.'

'Do you want to give up?' asked John, a twinkle in his eye.

'I certainly don't.' Her reply was emphatic.

Once again she could feel her interest aroused, in spite of the frustration.

She knew she would have to come back to Moffat, whether young Mr Jameson could help her or not.

She couldn't rest, now, till she found out what had happened to Rose Fielding.

'You look just as you did when I first saw you,' John teased Helen, 'like a terrier hot on the scent!'

'Oh!' The girl felt slightly disconcerted.

'Shall we drive round Moffat and the surrounding area for an hour or so?' he asked. 'It will put off time till Mr Jameson comes home.'

'Yes, let's,' she agreed. 'I've never been here before, and it all looks very lovely.'

It was quiet and restful countryside, with gentle hills and beautiful views.

Helen was enchanted with Moffat itself. John parked the car in the centre of the small town, and she gazed in shop windows at the handwoven tweeds and lovely soft lambswool sweaters.

'It's a good job the shops are shut,' John teased, 'or you would be spending all your money!'

'I expect I would!' Helen laughed.

But the hands of the clock were creeping up to three o'clock, and they decided to return to Foxholes Cottage.

Colin Jameson had just arrived home, a broad stocky figure with a weatherbeaten face and curly brown hair.

'This lady and gentleman are looking for people called Fielding who used to live here,' his wife explained. 'Weren't the last people called Clark?'

'That's right. They moved away to Cumberland, though. You must be going back a long time.'

'Forty years,' his wife informed him, and Colin Jameson laughed heartily.

'Before our time, I'm afraid. Now, let me see . . . I remember a family being here before the Clarks. And I think there was an older lady here, all by herself, when I was a boy. I never really knew this area well.'

'If you could remember anything at all,' Helen put in hopefully, 'that might help me.'

'Maybe I could find out the name of the old lady, and the young family, though it would take a wee while.'

'Oh, but Colin . . . ' his wife began,

then broke off abruptly. 'I'm sorry. Of course you'll find time to help.'

'No, I can see you're busy,' Helen said firmly. 'I'm thinking of coming to Moffat for a few days. I could try to find out for myself, if you could just give me an idea as to who would be likely to remember that far back. Has anyone stayed round here for a very long time?'

'Well, there's an old man at the farm nearby. His daughter and her husband run the farm now, but he lives with them. If anyone can remember, he will.' Colin Jameson smiled helpfully.

'Thank you,' Helen said gratefully.

She turned to John.

'Don't you see? Someone who has lived here for years, and seen people come and go, would probably remember them quite well.'

'I suppose so,' he replied, with a marked lack of enthusiasm.

Helen glanced at him briefly as they got back into the car.

'Do you want to try the farm now, or

shall we call it a day and go home?'
John asked.

'I think I'd better come to stay in Moffat, so that I can follow up any trail.'

'Yes, I heard you say so,' said John.

'Look, John,' Helen said sharply, 'either I do the job properly, or not at all. It would be useless to come all this way to ask a few questions now and again. I could never search properly like that.'

'Oh, I know,' he agreed. 'It's just that you'll be trying to manage on your own . . .'

Helen was tired and spoke hastily.

'What's wrong with that?' she returned crossly. 'We've been over all this before. You mustn't try to fight my battles for me, John.'

'Sorry.' His tone was stiff. 'I thought you appreciated my support.'

'I do! Only . . . when you can't help, don't try to stop me doing what I've undertaken to do.'

'I'm sorry. I was only trying to do

what was best for you. However, I won't interfere again.'

They were rather silent on the way home, and Helen felt a barrier had grown up between them.

'Thank you for taking me,' she told him, when they eventually got back.

'That's quite all right.'

'I . . . I'll let you know what I'm going to do. I'd better come and see your Aunt Nan again before I leave.'

'She'll certainly want to see you. Helen . . . ' John called after her, as she wished him goodnight.

'Yes?'

He looked at her standing there, already impatient to get on with the job on hand.

'Nothing. Goodnight, my dear,' he said gently.

He got into the car and drove away.

Helen felt depressed when she went to bed. It was going to mean considerable effort for her to start searching in Moffat, even if she did feel an urge to go on.

But she would not have John to encourage her.

★ ★ ★

Helen handed in her notice at the airport, feeling that she couldn't expect them to allow her leave of absence to continue her search.

If she found Rose Fielding quickly, she would have to think carefully about her own future, she decided.

She wrote home to her parents, explaining things as best she could. Then she made plans to go to Moffat after she had completed her notice.

Mrs Cathcart was sorry to lose her.

'Och, I'll be anxious about you, Helen, till I know you've settled somewhere. How will you find digs?'

'I don't know.' The girl shrugged. 'I think I'll have to find a small boarding house first of all. Moffat is such a nice town, though. There's sure to be somewhere suitable.'

'Well, any time you can manage, do

come back. Your room will be ready. And if you have to give up your search, then come straight here.'

'Thank you.' Helen bent to kiss the homely woman who had been so kind to her.

Moira, too, was disappointed to see her go.

'Oh, Helen!' she said, with dismay. 'I'm going to miss you!'

'What about Alan?' Helen teased. 'You've got him now, haven't you?'

'Yes,' the other girl said softly. 'I'm going to Kilmarnock on Saturday. Couldn't you come with me, and see the McBrides before you go?'

'I'll be glad to,' Helen told her. 'I was wondering how to get in touch with them.'

'I was hoping you'd be my brides-maid when Alan and I can get round to planning our wedding,' Moira contin-ued shyly.

'Well, I'm not going all that far away. I'll be glad to come back for that!'

'I can hardly believe this is all

happening to me,' Moira continued. 'It's been like living in another world since you came.'

'Am I responsible for all that?' asked Helen, her eyes twinkling.

'If it hadn't been for you, I'd never have met Alan,' her friend said seriously.

But John Segreave looked annoyed when he knew Helen's time was taken up on Saturday evening.

'I was hoping we could go out together,' he told her, so obviously disappointed. 'I've booked a table, and I thought we could go to the theatre. However . . . '

His voice trailed off and Helen felt a pang of disappointment too. She would have loved a night out with John, but she couldn't break the arrangements with Moira and the McBrides.

'I'm sorry, John,' she said, 'but I did want to see the McBrides and Moira before I left. When Moira suggested that we go together, I was only too pleased to agree. I didn't think you'd be arranging this.'

'That's all right,' he murmured. 'It was my fault. I tried to get hold of you earlier, but you weren't around.'

Later she saw him talking to Annette Thompson, and her heart sank a little.

Somehow the close friendship which had developed between herself and John was beginning to fade a little.

* * *

When Helen went round to see Mrs Segreave, just before leaving for Moffat, John was also at home.

'I'm feeling sorry I ever told you my real identity,' Mrs Segreave told Helen, her eyes full of apology. 'It's making such an upset in your life again. Giving up your job and going off to a strange place by yourself. It doesn't seem right for a young girl like you.'

She glanced at John who was frowning, and Helen felt they had been discussing this before she came in.

'I'm sure I can manage perfectly

well,' she said emphatically. 'I'm very glad you told me the truth. I shan't feel settled anywhere until I've made every effort to find out who should have that stamp album.'

'That old gentleman should never have laid such a charge on you,' said John. 'It wasn't the thing at all.'

'He didn't know it was going to lead to all this,' Helen protested. 'I'm only sorry he'll never know that he had a daughter. I'm sure he would have loved to know Mrs Segreave here, too. He was a charming person.'

'I hope you find his daughter, my dear,' Mrs Segreave said. 'Edith's girl. If you do, tell her Aunt Nan will give her such a welcome.'

'And if you don't, then give up and come home,' advised John.

'You don't seem to have much faith in my ability to fend for myself.' Helen stiffened, her anger growing.

'At least let me drive you down to Moffat again,' he suggested. 'I can help you find new lodgings.'

'Please, my dear,' Mrs Segreave broke in. 'I'd feel better about it if John took you there.'

'It's very good of you,' the girl replied gratefully. 'Thank you, John. I'll be very glad of your help.'

For the first time since her arrival, his face softened into a smile.

'That's all right, Helen. It's only a small contribution, after all. I realise you're doing it on our behalf, as well as your own.'

It was a wet, miserable day when Helen and John made the second trip to Moffat. The grey clouds which poured rain over the hills seemed dark and ominous.

Helen had confined her belongings to two cases, and Mrs Cathcart had offered to store a few things for her till she was settled.

She had received a letter from her parents, hoping she would find time to go down to Bolton.

'I doubt if I'll manage that before Christmas,' she confided to John.

He said nothing but she remembered how keen he had been to meet her parents over Christmas. She wondered if she ought to remind him.

But though he was being helpful in every way he could, she still felt that the relationship between them was not the same as before.

Perhaps the dull day had something to do with it, Helen thought despondently.

She thought of the happy day she had spent with Moira and the McBrides in Kilmarnock, and could not help envying Moira a little.

In the face of Alan and Moira's obvious happiness, Helen felt her own life to be empty and lacking direction. But she put her problems to one side and joined in the gaiety of the occasion.

'Moira's a fine lass,' the older woman said contentedly. 'Thank goodness Alan is settling down at last.'

Alan had seemed much more mature now that he and Moira were planning their wedding, and he had time for a quick word with Helen before she left.

'I'm sorry, Helen,' he told her gently.

'For what?'

'Making a nuisance of myself. I can see now that I must have been an awful bore to you.'

'You weren't at all, Alan. But I'm glad you and Moira are so happy.'

'I'll dance at your wedding, too,' he said, his eyes twinkling.

She coloured a little.

'That's far away, Alan. You'll have plenty of time to practice!'

She was thinking of this and other things as the car swished along the wet roads.

Such a lot seemed to have happened since she came North in September . . . such a lot in a fairly short time. It was hard to take it all in.

★   ★   ★

As Helen had predicted, it didn't take long to find a suitable boarding house, though she knew she would have to find a job of some kind if she had to stay there for very long.

Once again she had to face the question of money, but she kept this to herself and assured John that it was all she could wish.

'It's like being on holiday again.'

'Well, that's one way to think about it,' he agreed.

The skies had cleared a little, and the fresh wind made the little town look clean and well-cared-for.

'I shall enjoy it here,' went on Helen. 'I'll start by visiting that old gentleman at the farm near Foxholes Cottage . . . the one Mr Jameson told us about. Let's hope he's got a good memory, then maybe I'll have success very quickly. He might have kept in touch with the Fieldings after they left, and be able to put me on to them straight away.'

'That's true,' agreed John. 'But don't hope for too much.'

'So there's no need to bother about me, John,' she reassured him.

'Well, if you're sure you'll be all right,' he said reluctantly.

'Of course I'm sure.'

He glanced at his watch, and she thought about his journey home again.

'You'd better go now, John. You've got a fairly long journey back.'

He straightened up.

'All right. If that's the way you want it.'

She went out to the car with him. Before he climbed in, he gave her a quick kiss. Then the car seemed to leap forward, and he was gone in a flash.

Helen felt a loneliness such as she had never known before.

The boarding house was warm and cosy, but she felt cold inside. Nothing had prepared her for this feeling of desolation. It was as though something had gone right out of her life.

Did John really care about her, or did he only feel some sense of responsibility towards her?

She thought of Annette Thompson. Sometimes one did turn again to childhood sweethearts after being friendly with other young people. It was part of growing up. Perhaps after going out with her, he would take up his friendship with Annette.

Helen was sure that Annette really cared for John and he surely felt some affection for such a beautiful young woman.

Helen felt very depressed as she tried to sleep in her strange bedroom. And it was many hours before she fell asleep.

Miss Rose Turnbull . . .

On Monday afternoon, after settling in at the boarding house in Moffat, Helen walked over to Longclose Farm, near Foxholes Cottage, to ask if she could speak to Mr Dodds.

She had called on the young owners of the cottage again, to ask the name of the old gentleman Colin Jameson had mentioned.

'Old Jake Dodds,' said Colin. 'He's well into his eighties. Some say ninety, in fact, but he's very spry for his age.

'His son-in-law runs the farm with the help of a grandson, but Mr Dodds still likes to do his bit around the place. He would know all the people who've lived here at Foxholes, I'm quite sure.'

'You don't think he'd mind my asking questions?' Helen asked hesitantly.

'I think he would welcome you,' said

Colin with a smile. 'He likes company.'

Helen thanked the Jamesons, then made her way over to the farm.

Walking tentatively into the yard, she heard sounds of activity coming from one of the outbuildings.

Shyly she knocked on the half-open door, and a youngish woman peered out.

'Mr . . . Mr Dodds?' Helen asked.

'He's in the kitchen.'

'I was wondering if I could have a word with him. My name is Helen Ferguson, and I think he could help me.'

'Are you from one of the Ministries?' the woman asked bluntly.

'Oh, no!' Helen grinned. 'Nothing like that. It's personal business really. Nothing to do with the farm.'

The other woman's features relaxed into a smile.

'His pet hate is the Ministries,' she confided. 'I'm Nora Laverock, married to his grandson. Grandfather will likely be having a wee nap after his dinner.

'I was just thinking I could do with a cup of tea, so I hope you will join me, Miss Ferguson.'

'Won't I be disturbing Mr Dodds?'

'He'll wake up soon enough when I put the kettle on,' Mrs Laverock said with a twinkle. 'He likes his cup of tea.'

But old Mr Dodds was already awake when the two women walked into the kitchen.

'Hello, Grandpa. This young lady has come to see you. Miss Helen Ferguson.'

The old gentleman eyed her shrewdly as she shook hands.

'John Ferguson's lassie?' he asked. 'John Ferguson that went to Australia . . . or maybe it was New Zealand?'

'No, I'm from Ayrshire, though we moved to Lancashire,' Helen explained, looking at him with a friendly smile. 'I'm sorry.'

'Then you're a stranger,' the old man said heavily.

'I'm afraid so.'

She sat down on a nearby chair, indicated by Mrs Laverock, who began to put out cups on a tray.

'I've been over at Foxholes Cottage,' she told him, 'and Mr Jameson said you were the best person to see. I'm trying to trace a lady called Miss Rose Fielding, or she may be married by now. She'll be in her early forties.'

'Rose Fielding?'

Mr Dodds became wide awake now that his mind had fastened on a problem.

* * *

'I believe there would be a Mr and Mrs Fielding, with their daughter, Rose,' Helen went on. 'They lived in Foxholes Cottage about forty years ago. Mr Jameson said you might remember them, and know where they had gone. The farthest back he could remember was an old lady living on her own, then a young family . . . '

'He means Miss Morrison,' put in

222

Mrs Laverock, 'then the Johnstones. I don't remember anyone called Fielding, though.'

'Well, you're just a young lass,' Mr Dodds remarked. 'No, I'm thinking back. Foxholes had many a tenant.

'Ay, I remember the Fieldings. They were a quiet couple and kept themselves to themselves, but I never heard they had a daughter.'

Helen felt perplexed.

'A baby girl?' she asked. 'You don't remember any baby?'

'No. The only connection they had with a child was one they visited in the Children's Hospital, but it wasn't a daughter. Her name wasn't Fielding, anyway.'

'You don't remember the name at all . . . or where the hospital was?'

Mr Dodds put his hands to his head, deep in thought.

'Here's your tea, to help to oil up your memory,' Mrs Laverock said with a smile.

Helen took hers with a word of

thanks, though she felt disappointed again.

Just when she seemed within reach of her quest, it always slipped away.

'No,' Mr Dodds said heavily. 'I can't remember any more about it.'

'Oh!' Helen felt disappointed. 'Then you've no idea where the Fieldings went?'

'Oh, ay, I remember them going all right, though I've had no connection with them since they left the cottage. I heard they'd bettered themselves, though young Fielding . . . '

'Young Fielding?'

'Well, he was young then . . . in his thirties, younger than I was, anyway. I heard he had died suddenly and she went off to stay with a relative in a fine house on the other side of Moffat.'

Helen's eyes were full of hope again.

'You mean, just on the outskirts of the town? In the suburbs?'

'No. I think it was in the country, further up north. I only heard tell of them now and again, you understand.

She'll be an auld woman now, in her seventies.'

Helen's eyes caught Mrs Laverock's, and they both smiled. Mr Dodds considered other people old, but not himself!'

'You've been a great help, Mr Dodds,' Helen told him warmly. 'I'll have to ask around in Moffat then, and see if anyone knows Mrs Fielding . . . or Miss Rose Fielding. She's the one I wish to find.'

Mr Dodds frowned.

'Maybe she had a daughter after she left here,' he said at length.

Helen forbore to tell him that the daughter was an adopted child. No doubt Mrs Fielding would still like to keep private affairs to herself.

'Are they relatives of yours?' the old man asked curiously.

'She's the relative of a friend of mine who died. I've got a . . . a memento for her.'

'Ah. You'll be wanting to find her then. I'm sure we all like a memento of our own folks. I got my father's gold chain when he died and I'll pass it on to my grandson. Nora! Show the young lass my father's gold chain.'

'No, really . . . ' Helen spoke rather hurriedly, unwilling to take up more of Mrs Laverock's time.

'No, I'll get it,' the other woman put in. 'It will give him pleasure to have you admire it.'

Helen left about half an hour later, having duly admired the heavy gold chain.

She was a little further forward, she thought, as she walked down the lane from the farm.

Mrs Fielding would be in her seventies, so there was a good chance that she was still alive.

Seventy seemed young to Helen, after seeing old Mr Dodds with his good active mind!

Perhaps someone in Moffat would know her, and direct her to the 'fine house.'

Though what about Rose Fielding,

wondered Helen, as she walked along. Why was it that there had been no child at Foxholes Cottage?

Helen could find no solution.

* * *

Back in Moffat Helen found a small café and sat down to drink a cup of hot coffee before going back to her boarding house.

Her new landlady, Mrs Baxter, was a slender lady with neat grey hair. She ran the house like clockwork.

Helen did not feel like asking her any questions until she got to know her a little better.

For a while she sat musing. If she couldn't locate Mrs Fielding, should she try for a job in the town?

She might, perhaps, get a lead as time went on.

There was much she could do looking up old records, but it would all take time. And she couldn't afford to stay very long in Moffat without an income of some kind.

But she knew she was still tied to the quest she had undertaken. Somewhere there was a woman called Rose Fielding, a woman in her forties, who might be very glad of the inheritance her father had left her.

And might be even happier to find she had a loving aunt waiting to welcome her. That was the greater inheritance of the two . . .

Helen sighed and went to pay the bill for her coffee. She was tired again, but tomorrow she would start to look on the outskirts of Moffat for 'the fine house.' Surely someone would know which particular house she was trying to find.

The next week was a long one for Helen. She again tried the telephone directory, but when she phoned there was no-one called Fielding likely to be the one in whom she was interested, and she eventually gave up.

As the days went past, she found Mrs Baxter more willing to be friendly and realised that the quiet, dignified lady was rather shy.

'I had thought, when you came at first, that you might have been ill and needed the change,' she told Helen. 'You looked a little bit pale now and again.'

Helen laughed.

'I'm afraid my health is excellent, as you'll have seen by my appetite, Mrs Baxter. No, I'm looking for a family called Fielding who used to live out near Wamphray, but I'm having small success. They've moved somewhere north of Moffat, but that's all the information I have.'

'Fielding . . . Fielding . . . '

Mrs Baxter frowned, shaking her head.

'I don't remember ever hearing the name, Miss Ferguson, though I could mention it to one or two old friends, if you like.'

'That would be kind of you,' Helen said warmly. 'If I don't find them soon, I suppose I'll have to go back either to

Prestwick or home to Bolton. Or else get a job,' she finished, with a small laugh.

'What sort of a job?' asked Mrs Baxter.

'In an office, most likely. I'm a trained shorthand typist but I don't know whether I could find such a job in Moffat.'

Mrs Baxter shook her head again.

'I haven't heard of anyone needing a typist. But a friend of mine has a flower shop, and her daughter used to take the deliveries in a small van. But Julie's married now and living in Dumfries. She could do with someone to take her place.'

Helen's eyes grew thoughtful.

'If she wanted someone to help temporarily,' she began, 'perhaps I could help. I would need a little bit of practice driving the van, though. I took my test years ago, and haven't driven much since.'

Mrs Baxter hid a smile as she looked at the young girl, and wondered how many years ago she had learned to drive!

'Well, I expect you could manage,' she said with encouragement. 'Madge . . . Mrs Fleming . . . could sit in with you to see if you could handle the van.'

'That would be good,' said Helen. 'But how do I get in touch with her?'

'I'll phone her,' Mrs Baxter offered, and soon she was speaking to her old friend, explaining the position.

'Could you go round now, Miss Ferguson?' she asked.

'Of course. And please call me Helen.'

'Very well, Helen.'

It was a delightful little shop, and Helen was soon shown the ropes.

She spent most of the day taking down orders and helping with sales, as the job of making up bouquets was a very skilled one.

Mrs Fleming had been doing this all her life, and Helen was fascinated watching her nimble fingers at work.

In the evening they went for trial

runs in the small blue van until Mrs Fleming approved of the way Helen handled the van.

'There, you'll manage fine, my dear. It's fairly easy to drive these wee vans.'

'Yes, it's easier than I thought.'

The job helped to relieve her depression, as did a number of letters from John, Mrs Segreave, and several from home.

John was going to London for a week or two, and for a little while Helen felt more lonely than ever when she read that, but she cheered up when she read the other letters.

Now that she had the job, she had no intention of giving up her search again, so she wouldn't be able to see John anyway.

Did he miss her as much as she did him, she wondered, reading the letter again.

The letter was rather stilted, and she felt it had been written with difficulty. Perhaps it was just a 'duty' letter.

* ★ ★

Towards the end of her second week with Mrs Fleming, Helen was asked to deliver a large bunch of white and gold chrysanthemums to a house called Redlyn at an address she did not know.

'Where's this?' she asked Mrs Fleming.

'A few miles out in the country north east. I'll show you where. Now . . . where's the card? It's for Miss Turnbull, from Janette Lamont, with her most grateful thanks for a lovely holiday.'

Helen's heart leapt.

'Miss Turnbull!' she cried.

'Yes. Do you know her?'

Helen shook her head after a moment.

'No. At least, I don't think so.'

It was just that until she had found Mrs Segreave, she had searched so long for a Miss Turnbull that the name was practically engraved into her mind.

Redlyn was a charming house, built

of red brick, with a well-kept garden which looked tidy even at that time of year.

Helen rang the bell before taking in the flowers. She had learned to do that since she had, on past occasion, mistaken the address and perhaps disappointed someone who had already seen the flowers. Now she liked to make sure.

'Miss Turnbull?' she asked, when an elderly lady came to the door.

The lady smiled with apology.

'No, I'm afraid she's in Dumfries. I'm Mrs Fielding. Can I help you?'

As the woman spoke, Helen's heart beat faster. At last she'd reached the end of her search.

'Don't you feel well, my dear? Please come in.'

'No, I'm all right,' Helen told her, pulling herself together. 'I have some flowers for Miss Turnbull in my van.'

She hurried to lift out the large bunch of flowers. She could hardly believe she had found Mrs Fielding

. . . and Miss Turnbull!

'Is it Miss Rose Turnbull?' she asked, as she handed in the flowers.

'That's right, my dear. Did you wish to see her?'

Helen nodded, wondering what to do. She was on duty from her job, so she had no right to use her employer's time in questioning Mrs Fielding.

'Er . . . when will she be at home?'

'Next Sunday afternoon some time.'

'Could I come and speak to both of you then? My name is Helen Ferguson.'

'But of course.' Mrs Fielding's tone was warm. 'I'm sure Miss Turnbull will be happy to see you then. And don't worry. I'm sure she'll be able to help you.'

Helen nodded and turned away.

It was only as she drove away from Redlyn that she began to think about Mrs Fielding's remark.

How odd that she seemed to have accepted Helen's wish to talk to both of them as perfectly natural. And what did she mean by saying that she was sure

Miss Turnbull would be able to help? It was almost as though she had been expected!

Helen's thoughts also turned to Rose Turnbull. So she had taken her mother's name!

She remembered Mr Dodds saying that there had been a small girl in hospital whom Mrs Fielding had known.

He had said they had no daughter, and the child had a different surname. It must have been Turnbull, not Fielding.

It was now Thursday, with three days to go until Sunday.

Helen counted the hours, even as she continued to deliver flowers. She was enjoying the job, and was grateful to Mrs Fleming for taking her on.

On Saturday Mrs Fleming found her looking up bus time tables.

'Going on a journey?' she asked with smile.

Helen coloured.

'I'm going out to Redlyn tomorrow,'

she said shyly. 'You remember that house on the northern outskirts? I may know the people there . . . or relatives at any rate. I'm looking to see how I can best get there.'

'Why bother with the bus when you can take the van?' Mrs Fleming offered generously. 'Take it home with you tonight, and bring it back on Monday morning.'

'Oh, thank you,' said Helen with relief. 'That would be a help.'

★   ★   ★

It was Mrs Fielding who answered the door when Helen called on Sunday afternoon.

She showed the girl into a big airy sitting-room.

'Rose isn't home yet,' she told Helen, 'but perhaps we can have a cup of tea while we wait. I expect you'll want to see her about staying for a short while.'

'Oh, no.' Helen was mystified. 'No. I hope it won't take that long. As a matter of fact, I wonder if I can tell you about it first of all, Mrs Fielding.'

This time it was the older woman who looked mystified.

'We seem to be at cross purposes, Miss Ferguson. Perhaps it would be best to tell me first of all.'

Helen hardly knew how to begin, but managed to tell the older woman all about Mr Forbes, and her search for Miss Turnbull which had taken her to Ayrshire, and finally to Prestwick.

Mrs Fielding went very pale to begin with, then gradually became more and more absorbed in the story.

She showed special interest when Helen told her all about Mrs Segreave, and how much she would like to find her niece.

'If . . . if your Miss Turnbull is her niece,' finished Helen, 'Mrs Segreave will be so happy. She never wanted to lose sight of her sister's daughter.'

Mrs Fielding said nothing, but her expression was thoughtful.

'There's no need to hide anything,'

she said flatly. 'Rose is her niece . . . her sister's child.'

'Oh, I'm so glad, for her sake. She wasn't happy about the way her father had handled the situation. This is difficult for me, Mrs Fielding, because we're talking about someone who is as a daughter to you. Mrs Segreave's loss would be your gain.

'But she wanted me to tell you all about it, to show you why she hasn't tried harder to find her niece. She did come to Foxholes, but you had gone . . . '

Mrs Fielding nodded.

'I was told later that a lady had been looking for me. I remember very well. I remember everything about those early days . . . '

She was quiet for a moment or two.

'You say Mrs Segreave blamed her father?' Mrs Fielding asked heavily. 'But there was no need. The reason they asked Bob and me to look after Rose was because Miss Turnbull, as she was then, would have been completely incapable of taking on the job, as were her parents.

'In fact, her parents did their best to prevent heartache for their other daughter, Agnes, by taking all the responsibility on their own shoulders. There can be no blame attached to either of them. They were two of the finest people I ever knew — and the third is Rose herself.'

'I see,' Helen agreed absently, though she didn't know what heartache Mrs Fielding could mean.

'Edith's car accident was even more of a tragedy than you suppose,' Mrs Fielding went on to explain. 'Rose was born crippled, and for the first ten years of her life was in and out of hospital. She was the bravest child, and is the finest woman I have ever known. She can walk now, though with the aid of a stick.

'When her grandparents died, money was left to buy Redlyn for her, and enough to give her a small income for the rest of her life. She has turned the house into a Rest Home for people in need.

'Sometimes we have tired mothers who have been ill, and whose recovery is slow. Rose takes them all, but sees to it that the mother is well rested while the children are taken care of. We have one or two willing helpers, by the way.

'We also have elderly people who find themselves alone, and can't cope with their loneliness. We have young people who come after a broken love affair, like the girl who sent those lovely chrysanthemums. I thought you were one, by the way!'

Mrs Fielding laughed, and Helen joined in, but not too heartily. Perhaps it showed that her heart was rather empty at the moment . . .

'Things are getting rather difficult financially, but Rose is trying to earn money with home industries, small things which people can help to make.'

'But don't the Welfare people help?' asked Helen. 'I mean . . . is Miss Turnbull a trained social worker?'

'Oh, dear, no,' Mrs Fielding replied. 'This has nothing to do with organised social welfare. We only take in ordinary people who are finding things difficult, so that they can take a fresh look at their problems. I suppose you could say we look after people before they need help from Welfare workers.'

'I see,' said Helen, rather wonderingly.

'Rose has been in Dumfries today to see about orders for some of the home crafts she hopes to sell. She runs a small car which she has been taught to drive.

'I can't help feeling anxious when she's out driving, though I've learned to trust her ability to look after herself.'

Helen's thoughts were in a whirl. She remembered how Mrs Segreave had said that there had been very little money left when her parents died. Obviously, that was because her father had supported Rose, and tried to make the path of life as easy as possible for his crippled grand-daughter.

But what oddly secretive people they must have been to keep it all from Agnes!

She then thought of the stamp album.

Mr Forbes had left it to his sister-in-law and her family, as he had not known he had a daughter.

Was it fair that Rose should have her grandfather's money, and now this valuable stamp album from her father, while Agnes had received very little?

Helen's thoughts returned to the present as Mrs Fielding rose with a small cry of relief.

'Here she is now, Miss Ferguson.'

A moment later there was a light, rather uneven step in the hall, and Rose Turnbull walked into the room.

No More Partings

Although Rose Turnbull must be in her forties, she was easily the most beautiful woman Helen had ever seen.

Her golden hair was piled in a chignon at the back of her head, and she had large violet-blue eyes in a perfectly modelled face.

Apart from one leg which was still slightly crippled, she had a slender but good figure and wore a plain, well-cut suit.

'This young lady has come a long way to meet you, Rose,' Mrs Fielding said, introducing them.

'You're most welcome, my dear.' Rose Turnbull held out her hand. 'You must tell me all about it after tea.'

Helen caught Mrs Fielding's eye and realised, as had happened with the housekeeper, Rose Turnbull also thought her in need of help!

But she felt it would be wrong to correct that impression at the moment.

There was no doubt in her mind that Miss Turnbull was the rightful owner of the stamp album, and silently she hoped that she was doing the right thing for Mr Forbes.

If there had been no Rose, Mrs Segreave would probably have kept the album as a memento of her brother-in-law. But would Rose Turnbull keep it as a link with the father she had never known, or sell it, using the proceeds to help many more people?

Mrs Fielding now urged Helen to stay for a meal.

'Of course she'll stay,' Rose said firmly. 'I've had a good business trip, Aunt Edith. We shan't have to cut down nearly as much as I'd feared.'

'That's good. But Miss Ferguson isn't a customer, dear . . . if I can put it that way. She called to see you privately.'

'Oh, well . . . ' Miss Turnbull looked at Helen uncertainly. 'If you don't mind, can it still keep till after tea?' she asked. 'I would like to pop upstairs and wash.'

'Of course.'

Helen heard her slow progress up the stairs. As she listened to the dragging footsteps, she decided that she did not care if Rose Turnbull chose to sell the album. She was very sure Mr Forbes would have felt the same way.

His daughter had faced pain and disability with great courage, and had used her experience to help others, when she might so easily have become embittered with her lot.

After tea, Rose again led the way into the sitting-room, and Helen began to tell her story for what she hoped was to be the last time.

At first Rose listened with a small smile on her lips, then her eyes grew sober.

She leaned forward intently as she heard about her father's wish to leave his stamp collection to his only relative.

'He never knew about you, Miss

Turnbull,' said Helen earnestly, 'though I can guess how wonderful it would have been to him to have had a daughter, especially a daughter like you.'

The older woman flushed and dropped her eyes.

'I . . . I can't really take it in,' she said in a low voice. 'That my father died only recently. And that he and my mother became separated in such a way.'

There was a long silence in the room while the darkness began to fall outside. The bright fire threw shadows on to the delicate pale cream walls.

'So I can now hand over the album,' Helen said with relief. 'I shall write home and ask my father to post it to you, Miss Turnbull, by registered mail. There is a letter with it from your father, and a valuation. John Segreave would like to look at it, by the way, so perhaps you could let him see it. It's of considerable value as it contains some very fine, rare stamps.'

'But it isn't mine,' the other broke in.

'Surely you can see it isn't mine. It belongs to my aunt. My father asked you to find her, and give it to her . . . '

'But he only wanted her to have it because he knew nothing about you. She agrees with him, and she's quite right. She said her inheritance would be in finding you again — I've to tell you there's a loving welcome waiting for you when you meet her.'

Suddenly Rose was looking very white and tired, and tears slowly filled her eyes.

Mrs Fielding leaned forward.

'I think you've had enough for one day, Rose,' she said gently.

She turned to Helen.

'Where are you staying, my dear?'

'At a boarding house in Moffatt.'

'Then perhaps you would like to come here? We have a few spare bedrooms at the moment, though they don't remain empty for long.'

'That's very kind of you,' said Helen hesitantly, 'but I have a temporary job, delivering flowers. I suppose I'll have to give in my notice and go back home now that my task is finished.'

The girl's voice was rather sad. It would be difficult to pick up the threads of her old life again.

Rose had been sitting quietly, her face very pale, but she rose again to see Helen out.

'All this has been rather a shock,' she said, 'but I'll look forward to seeing you again.'

★   ★   ★

Later that day, Helen telephoned Prestwick and spoke to Mrs Segreave, telling her that she had found Rose Turnbull.

'Turnbull!' cried Mrs Segreave. 'But I thought she would be called Fielding.'

'Your father refused to allow her to be adopted — the Fieldings were only foster parents. There is a lot to explain, Mrs Segreave, I shall be back to Prestwick when I can conveniently leave my job, and tell you all about it.'

'I shall look forward to that, my dear. John comes back from London on Friday, by the way.'

'Oh!'

'Come as soon as you can, Helen. I'm very anxious to hear your news.'

Helen was able to leave for Prestwick the following Saturday.

Mrs Fleming had been able to look around for a more permanent replacement, and she was happy to allow Helen to leave.

'You've been a great help,' she told her. 'You filled the gap admirably, just when I needed you most.'

'I can return the compliment,' laughed Helen. 'You'll never know what a help you've been to me.'

'Here you are.' Mrs Fleming handed her a lovely bunch of flowers. 'This is for you. I've seen you admiring quite a few bouquets which you've had to deliver to other people.'

'Oh!' Helen coloured with pleasure. 'How lovely! Would you mind very much if I put them into a vase at Mrs

Baxter's? I can admire them there, as well as sharing them with her.'

'Not at all, my dear. Come and see me whenever you can manage it.'

The album had arrived safely from home, with a thankful letter from her family that her search had ended.

I hope we'll see you very soon now, her mother wrote. *We're all longing to have you home again.*

It would be lovely to be home, Helen acknowledged, as she packed her belongings.

She was staying overnight with Rose Turnbull, then travelling back to Prestwick the following day.

When she arrived at Redlyn, there was another warm welcome waiting for her, and for a moment Helen's eyes pricked.

It had been a long search, finding the real owner of the album, but she wouldn't have missed it for the world.

She had made quite a number of new friends, friends she intended to keep.

That seemed to her much more precious to her than the album.

★ ★ ★

Helen was disappointed to find that John Segreave was not at home when she arrived at Prestwick.

'Haven't you seen him?' Mrs Segreave asked. 'He went to meet you in Kilmarnock, thinking you were coming that way.'

'Oh, dear,' Helen felt deeply disappointed. 'I must have missed him.'

'Never mind. He'll come home soon enough, when he can't find you.'

But it seemed hours before John came back. By that time, Helen had had a chance to talk to Mrs Segreave, and tell her all about Rose Turnbull.

The older woman listened intently, exclaiming a little now and again.

'So that's why there was so little left after Father died,' she said at length. 'Though I wonder why he did not even leave me a letter of explanation. It would have helped so much.'

'Mrs Fielding said he didn't want you to feel responsible for Rose in any way, especially when it seemed as though she would always be a cripple. He didn't know then that modern surgery would one day help her to walk.'

Mrs Segreave sighed.

'Well, I feel as though a weight has been lifted off my spirit,' she said at length. 'I've misjudged my father so badly, blaming him for disowning his own grandchild, when all the time . . . '

'Rose felt rather unhappy that she was provided for so well, while you . . . ' Helen tried to explain, but Mrs Segreave took up the conversation again.

'Oh, but I had my health and strength, dear, and enough money for my needs till I married.'

'She felt you ought to have the stamp album, and wishes to discuss it with you.' Helen looked at her with a smile.

'I wouldn't dream of it,' Mrs Segreave replied flatly. 'I only wanted to meet my niece again. I'm looking forward to that so much.'

It was then that the door opened and John walked in.

Helen's eyes flew to him and she rose slowly to her feet.

'I'll go and make some tea,' said his aunt hurriedly, glancing from one to the other.

For a long moment John and Helen continued to stare at one another, then he put down his coat on a chair, where it slid gently on to the carpet.

'Helen!' he exclaimed. 'I've missed you.'

'I must have caught an earlier train.'

'No, darling. I mean, I've missed you so. Haven't you missed me at all?'

She nodded, and a moment later she was in his arms, where it seemed that nothing else in the world mattered.

'I was beginning to think you didn't really care for me,' she told him, huskily.

'And I felt you had to work out this problem of yours before I said anything else. You were so set on it.

'As a matter of fact,' he grinned a little sheepishly, 'I was afraid you'd think that if I prevented you from tracing Rose Turnbull, it was because I wanted us to have the album. You did remark once, that it might be mine some day . . . '

'I never thought of that,' said Helen, her eyes wide.

'So I can only be doubly thankful that you've worked it all out so satisfactorily. And now may I ask that at least some of your attention be cast in my direction . . . '

'In what way?' she asked mischievi-ously.

'In deciding whether or not you're going to marry me!'

There was real anxiety in his look while he waited for her answer.

'Only if you love me enough, John. To me that's awfully important.'

He looked at her incredulously.

'But I've loved you right from the first moment you walked in that door,' he told her. 'Why else do you think I did my best to keep you here . . . suggesting a job at the airport, and trying to help you find the people you wanted.

'I had no idea that they really were my people, you know. I only did it to keep you a little longer. Then I wondered about you and Alan McBride.'

'And I was jealous of Annette,' confessed Helen honestly.

'She's engaged to one of the pilots,' John told her, and Helen exclaimed with delight.

'That is good news. But she's so lovely, I felt you must be attracted to her.'

John turned her face up to the light, scrutinising her, his eyes dancing.

'Annette's only pretty, but you are the most beautiful girl I've ever seen. Now are you going to marry me?'

'Yes,' she said happily. 'Yes, please, John.'

'I've been very patient,' he told her,

after kissing her. 'I was beginning to wonder if it was a mistake, trying not to rush you. Yet I felt if I put a foot wrongly, you'd be hurrying back home to Lancashire, and I'd lose you entirely.'

'Oh, John!' She laughed with delight.

★　★　★

In the end it was decided that Mr and Mrs Segreave, John and Helen should drive to Moffatt to meet Rose and Mrs Fielding.

They had to wait till the following weekend when John and Mr Segreave were free at the same time.

Mrs Segreave grew increasingly nervous, alternatively full of joy at meeting her only niece for the first time, and apprehensive that Rose wouldn't care for her.

'She's probably every bit as nervous as you,' her husband told her at length, 'and thinking exactly the same things.'

'I'm sure you'll get on well with one another,' Helen assured her. 'You're both such nice people.'

She was feeling on top of the world at the moment, having written to her parents with the news that she hoped to bring John down to see them soon.

'We'd better not say we're engaged, darling,' she told John. 'Until they've met you, I mean. You do understand, don't you?'

'Of course. What happens if they disapprove of me?'

Helen grinned.

'They won't disapprove of you. But I think they know I'm able to run my own life, and choose for myself.'

'I keep forgetting that you can take care of yourself,' he teased. 'I'd like us to choose an engagement ring very soon, though, even if we don't officially celebrate our engagement till Christmas.'

'All right, John,' agreed Helen.

The visit to Redlyn was a wonderful success.

Helen felt her eyes pricking when Rose Turnbull came forward to greet her aunt, and after a moment's hesitation, Mrs Segreave held out her arms.

'You're so like Edith,' she said tremulously. 'This is a very happy moment, my dear.'

'Yes, thanks to Helen.'

Rose was aware of Mrs Fielding standing quietly in the background, and quickly drew her forward.

'Here is another Edith . . . my dear Aunt Edith, who has taken care of me since I was a baby!'

Mrs Fielding stepped forward to shake hands and welcome her guests.

When John was introduced Rose looked up at him with a friendly smile, then glanced mischieviously at Helen whose new happiness shone from her eyes.

'This is a specially happy occasion!' Rose smiled, and Helen blushed.

'Yes,' she admitted. 'There's certainly a lot to celebrate!'

After tea, Rose went over to the bureau and produced the stamp album, leafing over the pages so lovingly collected by Gemmell Forbes.

She and Mrs Segreave had discussed what was to become of it, and her aunt was emphatic that the album rightfully belonged to Rose.

'I think I'd like to keep it,' Rose said, showing them the rare stamps. 'Somehow I feel I now know quite a lot about my father, from looking at something he treasured.'

Helen looked at the album, then over to John and the family gathered together.

How very happy Mr Forbes would be, she mused, as John came over and put his arm around her shoulder.

In keeping her promise to the old man Helen had herself found a happiness she would never have believed possible.

THREE TALL TAMARISKS

Christine Briscomb

Joanna Baxter flies from Sydney to run her parents' small farm in the Adelaide Hills while they recover from a road accident. But after crossing swords with Riley Kemp, life is anything but uneventful. Gradually she discovers that Riley's passionate nature and quirky sense of humour are capturing her emotions, but a magical day spent with him on the coast comes to an abrupt end when the elegant Greta intervenes. Did Riley love Greta after all?

SUMMER IN HANOVER SQUARE

Charlotte Grey

The impoverished Margaret Lambart is suddenly flung into all the glitter of the Season in Regency London. Suspected by her godmother's nephew, the influential Marquis St. George, of being merely a common adventuress, she has, nevertheless, a brilliant success, and attracts the attentions of the young Duke of Oxford. However, when the Marquis discovers that Margaret is far from wanting a husband he finds he has to revise his estimate of her true worth.

CONFLICT OF HEARTS

Gillian Kaye

Somerset, at the end of World War I: Daniel Holley, unhappily married to an ailing wife and father of four grown-up children, is attracted to beautiful schoolteacher Harriet Bray, but he knows his love is hopeless. Daniel's only daughter, Amy, who dreams of becoming a milliner and is caught up in her love for young bank clerk John Tottle, looks on as the drama of Daniel and Harriet's fate and happiness gradually unfolds.

THE SOLDIER'S WOMAN

Freda M. Long

When Lieutenant Alain d'Albert was deserted by his girlfriend, a replacement was at hand in the shape of Christina Calvi, whose yearning for respectability through marriage did not quite coincide with her profession as a soldier's woman. Christina's obsessive love for Alain was not returned. The handsome hussar married an heiress and banished the soldier's woman from his life. But Christina was unswerving in the pursuit of her dream and Alain found his resistance weakening . . .

THE TENDER DECEPTION

Laura Rose

When Sophia Barton was taken from Curton Workhouse to be a scullery-maid at Perriman Court, her future looked bleak. Was it really an act of Providence that persuaded Lady Perriman to adopt her as her ward? Sophia was brought up together with the Perriman children, and before sailing with his regiment for India, George, the heir to the title, declared his love. But tragedy hit the family and Sophia found herself caught up in a web of mystery and intrigue.